Metaphorosis

July 2023

Beautifully made speculative fiction

Metaphorosis

July 2023

edited by
B. Morris Allen

ISSN: 2573-136X (online)
ISBN: 978-1-64076-261-9 (e-book)
ISBN: 978-1-64076-262-6 (paperback)

Metaphorosis
a magazine of speculative fiction
from
Metaphorosis Publishing

Neskowin

July 2023

When The Future Calls

Salena Casha

When Derek came down to breakfast, the sight of Savannah at the table stopped him cold. The derm-ate pod attached to his sister's left bicep pulsed with seafoam derm-paynt; she'd gone for *Crustacean Euphoria*, the one flavor that didn't leave an iron tang on the back of Derek's tongue. Except for the elite, no one on Earth had eaten physical food since 2100. The derm-ate feeder pods, embedded in their skin, were all they had now.

"How's work at the Mausoleum at the End of the Old World?" Savannah asked. "Anything, like, interesting recently, or you still cleaning glass?"

That's breakfast ruined, Derek thought.

He gritted his teeth as he rotated his shoulder. His joint clicked. Two days in a row now scraping graffiti off *The Vince Offer Series* at Infomercial Intersection. It didn't help that his dominant arm hosted his own empty derm-ate pod. The graffiti *had* been interesting, but as long as she called his place of work, the Museum of Anthropological Findings, a mausoleum, he wouldn't mention it.

"Aren't you supposed to be an adult and, *like,* get your own food instead of taking Mom and Dad's?" he asked, staring pointedly at her arm and then the front door.

She snorted. "You're the one living at home."

At least his assignment at the Museum gave him a reason to leave the house so he didn't have to hear, for the tenth time, about how what his parents really wanted was steak with bubbled butter in a pan. It didn't matter to them that the last cow had died well before Environmental Reconstruction. Before they were born.

He reached across the table and palmed through the remaining derm-paynt flavors. *Anthropoda Chiffon* and *Imperial Dulse.* Fancy scientific words for 'this will taste like ass and is made from either seaweed or ants'. They were lucky they could afford clean tenth-generation upcycled derm-ate filters. Derek had seen something about it recently on the news: how too many people died from stretching the pods beyond their allocated uses.

"I just don't get how you can watch the same dumb videos every day selling you shit you can't buy," Savannah said.

"You don't need to," he said and reached for *Imperial Dulse*.

If he'd been able to choose his job, which no one did, he'd have gone for his over hers every time. Savannah lived on the other side of Philly with a brutal set of roommates, all of whom waded knee-deep in toxic waste from nine until seven, collecting samples. Plungers sucking up earth muck and what little water there was left, to just spit it out somewhere else that told them it was *no good. Not ready yet.* They'd be lucky if the toxins didn't kill them in the process.

I'm on the cutting edge of post-environmental reconstruction, she'd said once. *They'll upload my words to students one day.* But what she avoided thinking about head on — something Derek thought about for her instead every day —

was that the exposure would be the end of her. And maybe, it wasn't worth it.

"You didn't always think the Museum was torture," he said. "Remember 4D?"

She rolled her eyes. "4D?"

"How you can pause a commercial and step into the frozen film frame and mess around. You know. When mom took us, back when we were kids, you went into a music commercial."

"Oh yeah," she said, distracted. Her forehead softened. "I think I tried a piano once."

They had 4D on Infomercial Intersection as well. He hadn't used it in ages, but once, on a particularly boring shift, he'd stepped into a Vince Offer frame. The bars of the recording had fizzled like carbonation against his skin and he had held a Slap Chop in his hand, the seamed plastic cold against his palm.

The memory lingered between them, like the echo of a touched key. Savannah cleared her throat.

"The other day, we were collecting samples on the South Side of the Delaware River, you know, the spot by the old Bristol plant, and Marina caught one of the testers just throwing them out. Dumping the mud we'd spent hours pulling right back into the river. It's all a hoax," she said.

"Did you see them do that?" he asked.

"Marina did."

"So you didn't," he said.

She glared at him and leaned forward. A pimple had crusted above her left eyebrow. She'd been picking at it. Whatever moment the 4D had given them was gone.

"If the Old Worldies had just done the right thing to begin with, we wouldn't be wasting our lives on pointless jobs. I don't get why it's our responsibility to fix their mistakes. We weren't there." She paused and leaned further forward. "We need to resist the tyranny of the past."

The room stopped.

The graffiti. *Resist the tyranny of the past.* Plastered red on Vince's face, on Derek's favorite infomercial of them all.

"Savannah," he lowered his voice. "What did you do?"

"You know it's true," Savannah continued. She took a sip of water.

"You're going to get yourself in trouble," he said.

What he really meant to say was she was making Environmental Reconstruction about herself, again. She didn't want to go on shoveling crap for the rest of her life and, while that was fair enough, it was also tough luck. Her discontent wasn't Derek's problem.

"Why? You going to run to your supervisor and put your only sister in jail?"

His jaw clenched. She was probably on a list already. Actually, *he* was probably on a list now. Typical Savannah, screwing everyone else's lives up without a second thought. He'd been an antibacterialist at the Museum for over fifteen years and wanted it to stay that way. There was something to be said for the comfort of those light-blocking windows, the dark walls, Vince Offer's voice echoing across micah.

She smiled to herself and stood.

"Thought so," she said. "Anyway, got to head out. Need to see if the water is unfucked yet or if we still need to drink filtered piss." She didn't push her chair in before heading to the door.

When he went to work that night, he filled an antique steel mug with beer to keep him company. Drank half before he reached the ruined display. What remained of the graffiti on Vince Offer's *Slap Chop* series was three days old now, and Derek watched Vince bob across the defaced screen, his head wavering in and out of the word *Resist*. His stainless white shirt glowed behind the carmine lens. What Derek would give to be next to him in the infomercial. Saying lines and smiling at the camera, palming the Slap Chop and showing America how to be skinny again. Eating stuff called tuna.

Derek looked at Vince and then down at the scraper in his hand. Savannah and her idiot friends trying to prove a point didn't bring the owners of the museum down to the floor to clean up the mess. He pressed the edge against the glass and began to scrape.

"Stop having a boring tuna, stop having a boring life," Vince said. He slapped his palm down on the white knob of the Slap Chop, the blades slicing dehydrated tuna into cubes.

Derek took another deep drink of his beer. The carbonation crystallized behind his eyes. Vince's teeth looked like bleached ceramic in the dark mica hall.

"Poor bastards," Savannah had said once. "Had no idea what was coming until it was too late. And now, we're so scared of what could happen if we try something new. There's no trust anymore."

"If you knew what was coming, I'm sure you'd do something about it," Derek said to the Vince on-screen.

If Infomercial Intersection was to be believed, Vince had been everywhere. Perhaps even at the same level as Hollywood stars. Everything Vince sold was meant to help people: the Slap Chop, the Schticky, the InVINCEable, the SHAMWOW. Make their lives more bearable. Derek watched as Vince continued slicing and dicing, iceberg lettuce this time. The crunch crisped and tingled the skin below Derek's ear. There was nothing the Slap Chop — and Vince for that matter — couldn't handle.

It was on historical record that plenty of people knew the climate crisis was coming and did nothing, but maybe Vince had been different.

Derek pressed down hard on the scraper's handle. The last *t* was almost gone now. From the smell of it, it was *Russet Scarlet* paynt. Probably stolen from their parents' supply. It flaked onto the floor at his feet.

Vince had pivoted to hard selling, throwing in a free cheese grater if you called in the next fifteen minutes. They'd even add in a cutting board for good measure — what a deal! Operators, Vince intoned, were standing by. Someone had scrubbed the number on the screen to show all zeroes. It blinked in half-assed binary. Somewhere, far off down the hall, an overworked water pipe clanged. Derek glanced briefly down the hall after the noise. Nothing moved except the light playing against black pitch from the activated Offer screen. He needed a walk around, a distraction so he didn't have to think about what Savannah had done. Derek raised his mug and took a long pull of beer. Swallowed. The alcohol was really hitting now, deep in the nerves of his hands.

He stepped away from Vince and felt, more than heard, the video pause. The silence dropped in on him like declining air pressure, and he continued past the Offer series to the videos he often skipped. He went through phases like anyone.

Wandering closer to the Joe Gray series, his fingers tripped across the screen. The infomercial activated.

"This is the only device on Earth that is truly hands free," Joe Gray said.

He wore an absurd headset with a suction cup attached to a 2000s mobile that kept the phone pressed against his head. Derek watched him, his stomach unfurling from its knot. He'd never touched a phone, never even thought about the object glued to Joe's head with any real curiosity. No one used Old World phones or numbers here anymore — thanks to the natural evolution of facial recognition from the 2000s, Derek could just leave a memory note or viz based on the image of a person's face in his mind. So this type of comms device wasn't a part of Derek's every day.

His eyes followed Joe Gray's lips as Joe spoke into the mobile. It was in every shot. Not a piano, but it was an artifact of the beginning of the technological revolution, the base of the exponential advancement curve. Way cooler than a piano.

Derek had tried plenty of Offer products, but not much beyond that. He was in untested territory. It would be a lie if he said he wasn't a bit drunk, a bit lonely. That maybe, it'd feel good to screw around and see how another Old World relic felt. Put his fingers over the numbers of a mobile pad for kicks. There was no one here. He wasn't even sure if his time at the museum would be numbered now because of what Savannah had done. If they knew, what did he have to lose? The only other option was just staring down a hallway at the end of the world, previously known as Philadelphia, in silence.

A thrill shivered down the back of his shirt. He walked to the Gojo Hands Free screen and looped behind the projection. It took him a few tries to remember the order of operations, but he finally managed to turn on 4D mode. Even though Joe Gray couldn't feel it, Derek moved carefully as he untangled the GoJo set from the frozen actor's ear.

His thumb grazed the keypad. He inhaled static. The mobile in his hand was still old enough to have letters above the numbers. 2 = ABC. He turned the phone over gently in his hand. There was a running joke about Old Worlders doing funny phrases for advertising purposes. Vanity numbers, that's what they were called, he remembered. They'd been plastered on billboards all across the corporate wasteland.

1-800-GOT-JUNK to get your old furniture to a landfill, pronto. Maybe 1-800-WEATHER to learn about the forecast. He laughed out loud.

Or even, 1-800-SLP-CHOP. That'd be a good one. He punched in the 1-800 and then 757-2467. Each push prompted a gentle ping. With the number complete, he clicked the button with a pine green, old-style handset on it and lifted the rectangle of plastic and metal to his ear.

The line began to ring, a tiny, sporadic jolt. They'd done the work to make it feel real, he had to give the museum credit for that, at least. He held the mobile a few inches away; he couldn't find the volume button. Apparently, Joe Gray liked it loud.

"Pick up, ya dumb Old Worlder," he said into the speaker.

This was *absurd*. He was about to end the call when he heard someone. At first, he thought it was coming from behind the screen. Grainy, a bit garbled.

"Slap Chop hotline, Bob here," the voice said.

Someone had definitely picked up. Derek's stomach dropped. He pulled the phone away from his ear. Stared at it as if he could see the sound waves coming straight toward him from the speaker box.

"Um, hello?" Derek said.

"Yes, hello?" Bob replied.

"Hello?" Derek echoed back again. His mouth had gone dry. There was someone there. A real someone. Shit.

"Yes?" Bob asked.

"Is this where," Derek tried to find the words, "I mean, do you sell Slap Chops?"

"Yup. That's what the hotline's for," Bob said. This man from the past sounded annoyed. Like he had somewhere to be.

This was ridiculous. Derek looked back down the hall.

"Okay. Wow. Okay," Derek said. His voice was too loud in his own ears. He ran his hand through his hair.

"How many do you want?" Bob asked.

"What?"

"Slap Chops. How many?"

"Do people buy more than one?" Derek asked.

"Sometimes."

"I don't need any," Derek said. He bit his lip, waited a beat. The alcohol tingled across his jaw and he pressed the phone harder to his ear.

"I'm from the future," he said. It came out in a whisper, but Bob heard it.

There was a huff on the line. "Look if this is a prank call, Slap Chop has a policy to take action against you people," Bob said.

"Look, no, sorry, I didn't mean to bother you, it's just, I'm a fan of Vince's. Watched his videos more than a few times," Derek said, trying to play it cool. "We've got a whole museum dedicated to them. Can I talk to him?"

"Vince Offer? You high or something?" Bob asked. "He's not in the call center."

Derek looked back down at the dregs of beer in his mug. Still cold, the froth staining the sides of the tumbler.

"No, not high, but I am a little tipsy," Derek admitted. That seemed, for some reason, enough of an answer to satisfy Bob.

"What did you want to tell him, futureman?" Bob asked.

Futureman. Derek smiled at that. Savannah would *hate* that.

Derek licked his lips. Breathed. "Um, I'm not sure."

"So let me get this straight. You're calling me. From the future. To talk to Vince. And you don't know what you want to tell him."

"No, no," Derek said. He looked back down the hall at the graffiti. Tried to remember back to his history classes of when the Earth started dying. Probably in Bob's lifetime. If Savannah had this chance, what would she do?

"It's going to sound crazy," he started, "but everything they're saying about the climate is true. We survived it, but it's not the same. We lost a lot."

Even though Derek wasn't sure what exactly they'd lost, he felt it in his bones sometimes. He saw it in the deep horizontal line in Savannah's forehead. The monotony. The lack of direction. Maybe that's what she'd meant by 'tyranny of the past', a past they were all still paying for today. Derek glanced back into the depths of the darkened hall. The pitch animated with the looping videos.

"Tell Vince," Derek said. His voice cracked.

The line had gone quiet. Somewhere in another hall in the Museum of Anthropological Findings, a digital counter clocked four AM.

"What the hell am I supposed to do with that?" Bob asked.

Derek wished he had the handless tool that Joe Gray loved so the phone didn't keep slipping down his slick palm.

"Just tell Vince what I said," Derek said again. "He'll know what to do."

Bob snorted. "He doesn't have two brain cells to rub together. And he won't listen to me. I mean, would anyone believe *you* if you told them the world was about to end?"

It took everything Derek had to keep the phone against his ear as panic crested through him like a wave.

"Probably not," Derek said. "I'm not anyone." His arm ached. He looked over at the GoJo, but didn't move to take it.

"Well, I guess time doesn't change that," Bob said. "I'm sorry, but I can't help you, bud. I don't like to rock the boat. Just come in on time, get my paycheck, and go home. No drama."

Derek took another long pull of his beer. He didn't know what to do with his hands except keep the phone glued to his ear, the past breathing down the line. Most of all, he wondered if Savannah would have done a better job. Been more convincing. Said the right words that would have changed history.

"Since you're from the future and all," Bob said. "Can I ask a question?"

"Sure," Derek choked out.

"Did it make a difference?" Bob asked.

"Did what make a difference?" Derek asked. He wanted to reach down the line and shake Bob. *This* was the difference. It was staring at him across centuries down a tenuous connection.

"The Slap Chop," Bob replied. "We've sold over a thousand so far. Did it make a difference in people's lives? I mean, you're calling me about it from, well, the future. So I'm assuming we're famous or something."

Resist the tyranny of the past. The remaining red paint glistened off of the Slap Chop's looping screen a few paces down from him. What Derek did know was posted below the digital display. By the end, Slap Chop had sold 50,000 of their devices. They did not end America's poor eating habits. He'd even heard that one had taken out the last surviving dolphin. Most, if not all, of the Slap Chops were pulled from landfills in the Great Recycling era that predated Environmental Reconstruction. They were dismembered and repurposed, the plastic powering early derm-ate filters that kept what was left of mankind alive.

"They definitely helped things along, one way or another," Derek said.

Bob mulled that one over but didn't press it. "Well, you sure I can't interest you in a Slap Chop or a Schticky?"

"You can schticky anywhere or anytime with anyone," Derek said. The quote from Vince's earlier product lines got him a shocked chuckle.

"What a weird day," Bob said. "I'm going to need a drink after this."

Yeah," Derek replied. "And think it over. What I told you. You could change everything."

Bob laughed at that. "You're not the only one trying to save the world, bucko and, if they can't, I sure as hell won't be able to." He cleared his throat and continued. "Gotta free up the lines for real customers. Take care, futureman."

A lump calcified in Derek's throat, the line cut, and with that, the past slipped back behind a silver screen.

Derek placed the mobile back on Joe Gray's ear. Slid the GoJo suction device back in place. He stepped out of the pixelated box. The static bubbled back across his skin and gave way to the clean, if antiseptic, air of the infomercial runway.

He unpaused the GoJo, watching Joe Gray jump back into a conversation with whatever actor played his mom. Gingerly, he sat down on the floor, crossed his legs in front of him and watched the video loop back on itself, over and over in the dark.

It couldn't help repeating itself. That was all it was meant to do, after all.

See Salena Casha's story "When The Future Calls" online at Metaphorosis.
If you liked it, leave a comment. Authors love that!
Remember to subscribe to our e-mail updates so you'll know when new stories are posted.

About the story

The initial germination of this story came out of a writing prompt from the NYC Midnight competition. If you haven't participated before, this is a sign from the universe telling you to do so. The upside is a writing competition like that will force you to write a relatively polished draft of a story within an allocated period of time, potentially for a genre you're uncomfortable with. Luckily, the prompt that started "When the Future Calls" included science fiction as the genre. While the story evolved dramatically since the initial draft (thanks in no small part to the tireless and detailed feedback of B. Morris Allen), I definitely encourage anyone who is trapped by writer's block — a claustrophobic space I find myself in more often than not — to give writing prompts a try.

Still, why climate change? Why Rich Pacte? Why Savannah? That all gets a little complicated but, essentially, my grandmother was recently hospitalized and when I was visiting her, her roommate watched an endless loop of jewelry infomercials. It was my own personal version of hell. But, the woman who chose to watch them clearly loved them. There was something about the videos on a loop that enthralled her. As I started the story, I brainstormed with my husband and he pulled up YouTube recordings of infomercials out there and led us directly to a few stars on the circuit such as Vince Offer, Joe Pedott, and Billy Mays, among others. Thus, Derek's obsession was born. I thought the infomercials would be even more compelling if it was a medium he didn't grow up with or understand and so, in looking toward the future, incorporating climate change for me was inevitable.

Climate change has been on my mind a lot recently and our tendency to want short-term solutions for long-term problems, to be absolved from our guilt, to buy "green" brands and say, "that's it, I did my part" which I'll be the first to admit I very much participate in. The news talks a lot about what future generations will inherit — and more specifically, what they won't — so I wondered a lot about what a new and changing world would look like where the New England neighborhood I call home would have the climate of Florida in the coming decades. I also thought, relatively cynically, about how even with scientists sounding the climate alarm since the 90s, if not before, we haven't really changed that much today. I wondered if our future selves would understand or despise us for knowing that we had known and did nothing about it. Or, if they'd hoped we were just naive.

Lastly, one of my favorite things to write is dialogue. I think dialogue, when executed well, really ramps up the tension of a story. I mean, just look at how Succession uses it to turn the dial up on its scenes. Bob came first as a character before Savannah and understanding their different voices, what they wanted, how they interacted with Derek, was the most gratifying part of writing this piece for me. Given that I'm influenced heavily by what I read, two recent finds helped give this story life, namely: Cormac McCarthy's set of novels *The Passenger* and *Stella Maris*. *Stella Maris* is written entirely in unpunctuated dialogue. The scenes don't move, it's just a conversation between a patient and a doctor. But it's explosive, it's effused with imagery. Even though the dialogue is untagged, you know exactly who says what. It's powerful to be able to live inside a voice so deeply, it speaks up from the page itself without the author having to describe it.

A final word on the process before I leave you. This piece didn't become what it was until it went through revisions. When I look at the first draft, it's unrecognizable. My husband reviewed it first; he's my most trusted reader and I take his feedback seriously. We ideated through the potential of multiple universes, the conversation between Derek and Bob, what Derek thought of Rich, of his parents. And then, B. Morris Allen provided insight that took this piece to its next level. My advice to writers out there is rewrite means rewrite. Some authors don't even look at the first draft of their manuscript before they begin the second. Be ruthless in your editing. Take that diversion to better understand your characters. Introduce a character, a hint of backstory, a new object. You might find a new theme or a powerful undercurrent that you hadn't noticed before. Maybe the story stays there, or maybe — as we learned — it comes back. All in all, it's where real writing happens. B. Morris Allen helped me take this story to somewhere both new and familiar, and for that, Derek, Savannah, Bob, and I are grateful.

A question for the author

Q: Why do you write speculative rather than realistic fiction?

A: Why do I write speculative fiction rather than realistic fiction, you ask? In general, I gravitate toward speculative fiction because it's my preferred genre to read. All my recent favorites run the wide gamut of speculative fiction from gentle magic realism to dark fantasy and horror. To get to know me and where my writing comes from, explore the worlds of Carmen Maria Machado, Marisa Crane, Emily St. John Mandel, Jennifer Egan, and Haruki Mirakami. They get it. Their stories and word choice gets it. How speculative fiction is sometimes the only way to describe our internal weirdness and spill it onto the page. How speculative fiction gives the space for rumination, for reflection, for, dare I say, speculation and, by its very nature, questioning. Speculative fiction allows me to twist reality into the shape that life feels like under my skin and show it to you and say, "See? This is what I was trying to get at all along." Recently, I worked on a piece about harassment in a workplace. I started writing it as realistic fiction, but the terms on which I could explain it to the readers didn't prove the desired effect, weren't helping me say what I was so desperately trying to articulate: that feeling of walking on eggshells, of being gaslit, of being disbelieved, so I wondered "what if the floor was lava and no one except the main character who was being harassed could see it?" And so, the story morphed into something speculative even if it was about a lived reality. My advice is, always, to let the story tell you where it wants to go.

About the author

Salena Casha survives New England winters on black coffee and good beer. Most mornings when hacking away at a piece in progress, she worries if "writer" is a title she can apply to herself. Whether it's an apt title or not, she's happy that by some kismet combination of SEO and love for science fiction, you've found your way to this story. In her professional life, she has been a literary agent, a math textbook editor, an English teacher, and an IT manager. When not reading, or working, she trains for marathons and tries to remember to stretch. Usually, you'll find her writing at your local brewery.

salenacasha.substack.com, @salaylay_c

When the Oracle Speaks

Albert Chu

One year after the war's end, the royal court welcomed a hundred orphan boys into our ranks. They flew into the city's spaceport by shuttle and proceeded up the hill on the backs of the court's own palanquin-bearers; upon entering the palace grounds, they received the speeches and banquets we held in honor of their noble suffering. The boys, hailing from the kingdom's most war-torn moon, had lost everything, but now their days of hardship were over. They had become esteemed wards of the House of Hassam.

After a few days, though, people in the court whispered of something else. The cooks and dressing girls repeated the same rumor: *Did you hear? One of the new boys can see the future.* The ministers and generals, who should have held themselves above idle gossip, indulged in speculation: *If this is true, could the boy be of use?* And everyone wondered how the king might act. We all knew his strength was the House's strength. If the boy possessed some special power, my father would take him.

So I never had any intentions of turning the boy to my side. I was just curious.

I found him sitting on a bench in the middle of a courtyard, surrounded by onlookers. It was another rainy day, and all the aristocrats had a servant beside them, shielding their heads with an umbrella. Some pretended to write calligraphy or paint—the perfect image of artful nobility, honing their talents as the rain fell around them—while others just stared.

I took in this scene from the colonnade which circumscribed the courtyard. "Come," I said, and my servant chaperone opened my umbrella. "I'm going to talk to him."

We left the colonnade's shelter and entered the courtyard. The boy didn't appear special—he was skinny and looked around the same age as me, and the only thing unusual about him was his uncovered head. Rain plastered his thick, reddish curls to his forehead. They'd be a frizzy mess later; I wrinkled my nose at the thought of it.

Instead of looking up as we approached, he only stared at the rain hammering the surface of the courtyard pond. He'd been doing that, it seemed, all afternoon long. My servant and I stood there, waiting, until the silent lack of recognition grew irritating. Finally, my servant spoke: "Prince Meira Pashel em-Hassam wishes to speak to you."

The boy turned around. His eyes swept over me—my jeweled coat jacket, inlaid with silver; the ceremonial lightgun at my belt; my coiled black locks, cascading to my chest and lustrously shiny. The regalia of a prince was designed for impact. But his face betrayed no emotion—not fear, nor awe, nor muffled resentment—none of the familiar reactions.

As if he expected it all. My irritation grew.

The boy didn't bow, but I refrained from comment; I'd already conceded enough conversational power to this commoner. Instead, I said, "You look wet. Would you like an umbrella? My servant can fetch one."

He shook his head. "I like the rain. It's nice on my head."

The word the boy used for 'rain' caught my attention—a formal construction, not the colloquialism that everyone in the city used. I remembered why he was here. We were both Artani, but I had been born on this moon, Artan itself, while he, like the rest of the orphans, was from Eshtan. Once the crown jewel and proudest province of the House of Hassam, now a dead moon, bombed to a ruin by the Samandirans.

The boy lacked etiquette, but not only was he my House's ward, he'd also lost his parents to the Artani people's mortal enemy. I could hardly reprimand him. So instead, I said, "Welcome, in the name of the House of Hassam, to your new home. Our hospitality is yours to command."

The boy responded to my generosity with only a turn of his lips. I had expected gratitude, and having not received it, I was off-balance. His lips slid back into a level line, and his flat, even stare did nothing to help me regain confidence. I had never spoken to someone like this before.

"What's your name?" I asked.

"Iuno."

"Iuno," I repeated. "Well, everyone is talking about you. I wanted to know more for myself. About your powers."

He sat there, his hands folded in his waterlogged lap, and waited.

My smile grew pained; I'd lost patience for subtlety. "Please tell me about them. How far do you see? What is it like? Can you tell me if someone will be dead in a year, or which side will win a war? Are you ever wrong?"

"That's a lot of questions." Iuno pushed some of his dripping hair out of his eyes.

"And to say that you can see the future is an extreme claim." *And I'm your prince.* "Indulge me."

"If you insist," he said, and I smiled harder to stop my nostrils from flaring. "In the morning, I see everything that I will live through that day. At night, I sleep, and when I wake, it happens again with the new day's knowledge. It's actually fairly simple."

"You must see one of many possible futures, then, perhaps the most likely—"

"No." Iuno spread out his hands, as if to apologize for his gift. "I see exactly what will happen. I am never wrong."

I narrowed my eyes. Was this what he had the entire palace believing? Did people think my father might desire this boy's power?

"I'm going to choose a number." I crossed my arms and allowed myself a small smile. "Zero or one. Which will I choose?"

"Zero." He didn't hesitate.

"Well, I choose one. Didn't you say you were never wrong?"

And then he began to laugh.

For such a small boy, he had a very loud laugh, and it was remarkably ugly. He wheezed like a decrepit minister a week from death. His cackling was unnaturally pitched several tones higher than his normal voice. He occasionally snorted.

Nobody in the courtyard pretended to practice the arts anymore. Aristocrats held their pens frozen in mid-stroke, and servants dropped their umbrellas to cover their mouths with both hands. After those umbrellas bounced off the cobblestones and clattered to rest, nothing moved but the endlessly falling rain and Iuno, who still shook with laughter.

Eventually, he stopped. He reached into his pocket, withdrew a scrap of paper, and handed it to me.

It, like Iuno himself, was completely soaked; I held it delicately to prevent it from dissolving in my hands. After reading a few lines, I understood.

He had transcribed our entire conversation. The trap that I thought I'd laid so cleverly stared back at me from the page: *didn't you say you were never wrong?*

I read the note twice, three times, while the stillness held around me. Everyone marveled at the audacity of this orphan boy, who, by laughing in the face of Prince Meira Pashel, had surpassed even the latitude afforded to a guest. They wondered what I might do to him.

I crumpled the paper in my fist and squeezed it to pulp. "Come with me."

We walked out of the courtyard, followed closely by my confused chaperone. Under the stares of the gathered aristocrats, we passed through the colonnade and into the warm, sunlamp-lit atria of the palace itself. I led him up the silver escalator to the floor with my suite, and when I reached my door, I turned to my servant. "Bring some hot towels for my guest and enough tea for both of us. You may leave after doing so."

The servant wiped the confusion off his face and bowed; he understood my request for privacy well enough. "Yes, Prince Meira."

When he left, I glanced down at Iuno's sandals. With each step he took, he pressed rainwater out of his drenched soles with a wet, squelching sound. A trail of damp footprints followed behind him. "Take those off before your step inside," I said, "and wait here. I'll get you something to dry your feet."

A few minutes later, Iuno, no longer dripping, sat next to me on my divan. The towels the servant had provided lay in a crumpled corner outside my washing room's entrance. He'd changed into one of my spare tunics; the lavender scent of the palace maids' laundry detergent clung to him. We both held cups of tea in our hands.

"It never rained on Eshtan." Iuno held his cup close but didn't drink, content instead to let his eyes bask in the steam.

"I knew, today, that I'd feel it for the first time. But I didn't expect how it could mingle with sweat and sting your eyes. Or how it makes the air smell like dirt."

He spoke of his dead home—his parents' grave—so lightly that I wondered if he missed it at all. Everyone knew how to speak to a victim; everyone could console a poor orphan for his loss. But he was different, and scripted gestures of nobility rolled off of him.

When he turned to face me, his steady gaze bordered on a challenge. "You didn't punish me, like they all expected you to."

"No." I ran my fingers around a groove in my teacup. "I didn't."

However aggravating his laughter, however angering the exact correctness of his transcription, he was right. I had told him to prove he saw the future without error, and he had done so. How could I fault him? Perhaps he had laughed so freely because he had seen, when he opened his eyes this morning, that I would not punish him.

Still, I needed to ask one final question. "You lied," I said. "You gave the wrong answer. You say that you know the future, but how can anyone trust you?" How could *I* trust him?

Finally, Iuno took a long sip from his cup. Then, he said, "You wanted to use me to prove that if you knew the future, you could change it. You weren't interested in the truth. I'm not a trustworthy tool, but if you want the truth, I'll give it."

Was he challenging me at all? He showed no attention to the protocols of etiquette and hierarchy; he said exactly what he meant, without hiding his true meaning. What if it wasn't some inscrutable gambit? What if he just wasn't playing the game?

As we finished our drinks in silence, humid air creeped into the room from my suite's open bay windows. Rain blanketed the entire city, and from our vantage point, we could see the swollen, frothing banks of the Azure River, its winding course cutting the city in half.

Iuno placed his empty teacup down. "Thank you for the tea, Prince Meira."

I held up a hand to stop him from leaving. "Before you go," I said. "I have a proposal. Instead of living in the common rooms with the other orphans, how would you like to make this your home?" For a moment, I wondered how to package my motivations—but I had tried, fruitlessly, to maneuver around Iuno for the whole day, and I was tired. "I never understood the tradition of princes having companions. There are dozens of boys from noble families who can fight or paint or just look pretty. The thought of randomly choosing one of them always bored me. But you're different."

He waited before answering; I willed myself to release my held breath. Then, he nodded. "Thank you, Prince Meira," he said. "I accept."

I chuckled. "Well," I said, waving a hand, "if we're going to be friends, you can't call me by my title. My name's Ahpa."

"All right." He smiled—something shy and genuine, the first time I'd seen that expression on his face. "Ahpa, then."

We grew older. While the commoners kept their hair short, the palace stylists knew to trim a noble's hair only enough to prevent split ends. Eventually, my black curls cascaded down to my hips.

Iuno remained my companion. Some ministers, trying to gauge his usefulness, managed to corner him and press him with questions, but they always left disappointed. He had no power; he had no more ability to change the future than an ordinary person had to change the past. And if my father himself ever made a move for him, I never saw it.

We came to know each other. Iuno learned of my taste for dates, and on some afternoons, he surprised me with a plate of them, fresh from the market. "The merchants sell these only rarely," he would say, "but I saw that they'd have them this morning, so I walked down the hill to get us some." And while we finished the plate together on my divan, we talked. Sometimes about idle court gossip or the latest minister to embarrass himself in some political blunder. Sometimes about our favorite pieces of classical poetry. Sometimes about the war.

"On Eshtan, did you ever see them?" I once asked, between bites of date. "The enemy."

He nibbled at his own dates, taking as long to finish one as I did to eat three. "I did," he said. "They occupied my village for some time."

"What did they do?" A scene of Samandiran brutality from the propaganda holovids flashed through my mind.

"Nothing exciting. Mostly, they were ordinary people." Even when speaking of the soldiers who'd killed his parents, his voice betrayed neither anger nor sadness. "They were only there at all because they'd been ordered."

I scoffed. "Samandiran High Command invaded Eshtan in a surprise attack a full day before they bothered declaring war. They killed millions of colonists like you. Shouldn't they pay?"

"How?" he asked. "Another war?"

I blinked. Officially, the war had ended when my father, having turned the tide against Samandir, forced them to sue for peace. But everyone in the court knew that the ceasefire's true architects were key ministers in my father's council; he, to the contrary, had wanted to press his advantage and continue the fight. In recent months, as the peace grew stale, I'd overheard conversations where generals cursed those ministers and whispered their longing for revenge.

I shook my head. "I didn't say that. Still, how can you say they were just following orders?"

He shrugged, reached into his mouth, and fished out his date's pit, still shiny with saliva. "To me, everyone's following orders."

While I digested his meaning, he tossed the pit into our shared waste platter.

One day, some months later, the king convened a Great Circle, where the House of Hassam's princes, ministers, and generals gathered to vote on a question placed before them. A Great Circle could shake lives and turn the fate of the entire kingdom—but nobody knew why my father had called for one. That morning, I left for the Circle, walking blindly into the future, and in the evening, the Circle finished, I returned to my suite.

"Ahpa." Iuno lay belly-down on my rug, a book spread under his head. He craned his neck up to look at me. "Welcome back."

I stood a step inside the doorway and stared out the bay windows. My mouth was dry.

"It was an ambush," I said. After half a day in the throne room, silently watching the Great Circle unfold, the words spilled out of me.

My father had named half the senior ministers in the court, all ones who had pushed the House of Hassam towards a ceasefire at the end of the war. And he named one member of the royal family: Prince Meira Siushem em-Hassam, my eldest brother, his heir. All these men, he said, had committed treason.

His spies produced the evidence. In secret, the traitors had communicated with the Samandiran High Command to negotiate a permanent peace settlement. Its terms—when Meira Siushem took the throne, the House of Hassam would reduce its army to pre-war sizes, with the promise that Samandir would do the same.

A roar went up from the generals in the room. That, I knew, was an act, a front of outrage; surely my father had coordinated with them before convening the Circle.

"He asked us to exile the ministers." He'd been wise, not seeking execution— that was a step too far. "He called for us to disinherit Meira Siushem."

"And you voted to do so."

My mind stuttered. How was he so sure? But then—of course.

"I did," I said. "You've known everything I've told you since this morning."

"I have."

"But then why—"

Why not tell me? It didn't matter; my behavior in the Circle wouldn't have changed if I'd known the king's intentions beforehand. Everyone knew that Meira Siushem, naively chasing peace with the Samandirans, had lost, and there was nothing to do but vote for his disinheritance. Still, something sharp lodged in my chest—betrayal. Iuno hadn't told me.

"You're anxious," he said.

I had every reason to be anxious. With the throne's succession now in question, the king held the right to designate a new crown prince. By disinheriting Meira Siushem, he had invited us, his sons, to compete among ourselves for power, his favor, and a chance to become the next king. Some princes had fought in the war; they could exploit their military connections. Others had mothers from wealthy families; they could purchase influence. And some would eliminate their rivals with poison or lightgun fire—why not, if they could get away with it?

I had none of these advantages, and in a contest of violence, I was underequipped.

"I can see my future." I felt cold, but I resisted the urge to tighten my coat around my shoulders. "Prince Meira Pashel, a pawn in my brothers' succession game. Nobody will notice if I die."

I glanced down at Iuno and felt a spark of hope. I did have one advantage. "But you can help me," I said. "Your powers— I've always thought they can't *do* anything, but that isn't true, is it? When you go buy those dates, how do you ever know that the market is selling them that day? The knowledge just—happens."

"I only see that I buy dates, Ahpa. Then I buy them."

I shook my head. "Couldn't you use your powers to help me against my brothers? To give me access to this hidden knowledge?"

"No." He spoke this simple refusal without malice or spite, but frustration still gripped me. "You don't understand."

"What don't I understand?"

"I could just as easily share with you your doom. What if, one morning, I told you that you'd fall into a trap that day? What if I told you how you'd try to escape the trap, knowing that it was there, and still fail? You already tried to best the future once, Ahpa."

I stared at Iuno and remembered that day, years ago, when he had handed me that waterlogged note.

"Besides," he said, looking up at me with half-lidded eyes. "I have nothing to do with a power struggle between the princes of Hassam."

I bristled. "Even when my life's at stake?"

"It doesn't have to be. You could walk away, couldn't you? If you gave up your title, nobody would have any reason to quarrel with you."

I stepped backwards and curled my lip. Then, without saying more, I turned and walked into my study. The door clicked shut behind me, and silence, broken only by the heavy sound of my breathing, pressed in. My fist had clenched when I'd heard Iuno's suggestion of surrender, and slowly, I relaxed it.

Once, the king had also been a small prince, but when the incompetence of his brother, the reigning monarch, led us to lose half of Eshtan to the enemy, he had seized the future. He took the throne by force. He faced down Samandir's army, larger and better-equipped, and won. He did not surrender to fate.

Like my father, I had my wit. If I played the game carefully, gathering information, cutting deals, and devising plans, I could come out alive on the winning side—a respected prince, with armies and ships sworn to my banner. A small part of me dreamed of winning everything and wearing my father's crown. With Iuno's help or without it, I wouldn't surrender.

For one moment, I heard again his ugly laughter. I quickly stifled its sound.

For months, I had chased a secret.

The thread began with a corrupt customs official, a prime target for me to blackmail and a useful mine of information. One of the secrets he revealed: several months ago, a series of shipments, addressed to a place that didn't exist, had arrived at the docks by the Azure River. After he'd fabricated papers for them at the behest of an unknown party, they'd disappeared a week later.

Gradually, the thread unraveled. Irregularities in the hiring of several dockhands. Strange incidents when the city guard had cordoned off sections of the docks from public access, citing leaks of dangerous chemicals—obvious pretexts. Then the final clue, when I looked into all the companies which had recently filed dock work permits—one company existed only on paper, and they owned only a single warehouse.

When I staked out that warehouse, I found its entrance guarded by a pair of security automata. They were camouflaged to appear commonplace, but I knew better—these were of an elite line allowed only to members of the court. If any trespasser failed to give them the correct passphrase, they would attack, and only a battalion of armed men could hope to dislodge them.

I'd been thrilled. Some member of the court—perhaps even one of my rival brothers—had hidden something inside that warehouse, and now I only needed to crack it open. But at this final step, my progress stalled. I found no leads as to who exactly owned the warehouse, and I had no way past the security automata. I didn't have the passphrase, and without it, I was stuck.

"Something's wrong with you," Iuno said.

We sat across from each other on my rug, a chessboard between us. I'd carved the board and pieces myself and given them to him as a gift, many years ago. He had smiled when I presented them. "But Ahpa," he said, "you always win."

Now, he noticed my distracted play. I leaned backwards on my palms, sinking my fingers into my rug's deep pile, and released a long exhale. "It's a political matter. Nothing serious."

Though we still lived in the same suite and drank tea together, I'd regarded him differently ever since he'd refused to help me on the day of the Great Circle. I needed to secure my future, buffeted as I was by the instability of a House without an heir. What was the point in sharing with him my life of blackmail and backroom deals? If he wasn't helping me, what did he mean to me?

He grabbed one of his pawns at an angle and rubbed circles with the edge of its base against the board; wood scraped hoarsely against wood. "It looks serious," he said. "When you worry, you don't hide it well. At least around me."

"You must forgive me." I strained to keep my voice light; a prince did not allow a barb to offend. "I'm simply trying to open a locked door, but I lack the key. I didn't want to burden you with something that doesn't interest you."

"The key?"

"A passphrase."

"Yes," he said, and I looked up. The confidence in his speech, the flat set to his eyes, the relaxed slump of his shoulders—all familiar. Iuno never cared to feign surprise. "Would you like to know it?"

I stared at him.

"If you go to this door tonight, speak a passphrase, and gain entry, you'll know it's the correct one," he said. "What if you then return and give the passphrase to me? If, tonight, you do that, then I already know it. I can speak it now."

I saw, again, the circles that Iuno drew on the chessboard with his pawn, and I shivered. Still, I didn't understand. "But why help me?" I asked. "You said..."

"I said that I wasn't a tool. That if you wanted the truth, I would give it."

I tensed in apprehension. Was he warning me? Would the warehouse's contents not benefit me? But I couldn't let my doubts and questions dissuade me. I couldn't command the future with a fearful hand.

I exhaled and willed myself to relax. "Give me the passphrase."

He leaned forwards and whispered it in my ear.

After that, we continued our game without speaking; only the clack of pieces against the board broke the silence.

"Ah," he said. I had trapped him in a mate-in-five two turns ago, but he'd kept playing as if he hadn't seen. "You've won, haven't you?"

"I have."

He shrugged and tipped his king over. "I resign. Good game."

"You as well."

I stood to prepare for an excursion to the warehouse, and Iuno began to lay the chess pieces back inside the velvet-lined wooden case that I'd made with the set. Each piece slid into place with an insistent shush.

"After you come back," he said, "we should talk."

The light coming through my bay windows began to dim. Artan's ever-present rain clouds gathered to obscure the sun, and in a few minutes, rain would flow down the city's streets.

"All right," I said. "We will."

I left. Behind me, Iuno continued to place the chess pieces back into their case.

Outside the warehouse, the rain fell in sheets. It whipped the Azure River into a frenzy, and the waters responded with a hungry roar as they swirled past the dock. It pounded the warehouse's loading bay, transforming it into a marshy field of shallow ponds and rocky islands. Nobody, not even a dock worker, was about; the only things that moved were the automata. They paced back and forth, their armor caked with rust, and as they splashed through the watery field, droplets running down their limbs, they showed no signs of minding.

The shadow of a narrow alleyway enveloped me, hiding me from the automata. For a moment, anticipation and fear flickered in my chest, before I exhaled and snuffed them both out. I stepped out of the alleyway, protected by my umbrella. Espionage mission or not, I wasn't letting my hair get wet.

Both automata stopped and turned to face me; the rain filled the void of silence left by their stilled feet. I continued walking forwards with purpose.

One automata raised a hand, its rusted joints creaking as it did. It spoke, in a gravelly, muffled voice: "Halt."

That was the first layer of defense, meant to deter commoners who'd ignored the posted signs against trespassing and somehow wandered this far into the docks. I didn't slow. At first, the automata showed no reaction—those machine minds, hidden to me, recalculated and reconsidered. Then, as one, they both shivered. The illusion of rusted armor fell from them like an unclasped cloak, and now their carapaces, comprised of thousands of scales, gleamed in the rainwater.

"Provide validation." Its voice was as smooth and bright as a stream of molten metal.

I spoke the passphrase from memory: "Clouds aflame. Flower verdigris. In a summer field, a single stone."

The automata pivoted on their feet away from me, like a door swinging open, and I exhaled. "Validation accepted. Enter."

With the rain still pounding my opened umbrella, I walked past the automata's unblinking stares and entered the warehouse.

First it was quiet; then, the overhead lighting turned on with a droning buzz. I held one hand to my brow to shield my eyes from the unexpected brightness, while my other hovered by my lightgun. If there was a trap, they'd spring it now. But nothing moved, and slowly, I relaxed.

I saw what the warehouse concealed, and at first, I didn't understand.

It stood in the middle of the stark white floor, its matte black chassis drawing the eye like a dark stone in a field of sand. Six conical thrust nozzles dangled from the underside; now, they all pointed straight down, but I knew from the holovids how, in combat, they could turn and dance to make the craft fly in impossible ways. On either side of the nose, weapons bays brimmed with missiles, hexagonal ports arrayed like the speckles of a cobra, its hood spread, staring back at me.

A hover-bomber. And as I circled around it, I saw, emblazoned on its side, the emblem of Samandir.

Pallets of sealed crates lined the warehouse next to the hover-bomber; I pried them open at random and examined their contents. Short-barreled rifles, the same ones brandished by the enemy in both propaganda holovids and classified combat footage. Clean-pressed mustard yellow uniforms, the signature mark of Samandiran shock troopers. All the props needed to stage an attack in the city and have everyone in Artan think Samandir responsible.

Such an attack, ending in the loss of Artani life, would surely cause all-out war to resume. But who could have planned something like this? If I discovered the general or prince responsible for this plot, I could ensure they were executed tomorrow morning.

Then I felt the gaze of that hover-bomber, laden with deadly missiles, pressed against the back of my head, and my thoughts came to a choking halt. I knew the answer. Only someone with absolute power, above the reach of punishment, could have set this plan in motion. He had been forced to end his campaign before he'd destroyed the enemy to his satisfaction. Now he would have his glory and his revenge.

My father. I'd misunderstood him.

Night had fallen by the time I returned to my suite, and Iuno was sitting on the divan, a steaming porcelain teapot before him on the parlor table. My room's sunlamps, having dimmed with the onset of night, now emitted a warm, flickering glow. For a moment, I stood inside the doorframe and watched the teapot's shadow dance across the table. The rainclouds had parted; the whole city was visible from my suite. Houses and storefronts and lounges, each a point of light, cascaded down the hill to meet the river.

"You're back," Iuno said.

I sat beside him on the divan, my back straight, and accepted his offered teacup. As I told him what I'd found, the tea cooled in my hands. I didn't drink.

When I finished, I turned to face him. "You knew," I said. "You knew I'd find the hover-bomber there. You've known of the king's plot this entire day."

"I told you." His voice was quiet. "If you wanted the truth, I would give it to you."

Yes, as promised, he'd led me to the truth, and now I found it nothing but a burden. I could only submit to the king's authority and accept that he held the reins of the future, not me. His lie would send millions of Artani people to their deaths, and I could do nothing—nothing—

"No." I stood from the divan. "I won't accept this."

I paced from end to end of my suite, my naked feet padding against my rug's softness. The room's cramped size constrained me; my thoughts outgrew it. "No single member of the court can stop the king, but I can turn consensus against him. And to accomplish that..."

If the votes of a Great Circle fell in my favor, I could avert war.

"I will convince them," I said. "Is honor dead in our ranks? My father's plot makes a mockery of every martyr who died fighting the invaders." I set my teacup, now cold, on the table. "They'll see that my solution is the only path forwards. Quietly, so that no commoners are made aware, the king will surrender his rule to a council of regents. His plan must not proceed."

I saw it all clearly—how my words, carefully crafted, would sway them. How I would gain power over that room. How I could fight and win.

I opened my bay windows and braced my hands against the sill. The night air was cool on my face, and before me, the city's lights unfurled. Something surged inside me. Even as he descended into his own lust for war, my father tried to command fate, and now, I would do the same. I could accomplish something that men in the House of Hassam would speak of for decades to come—how one small prince, given a chance for greatness, had defied a king and prevented war.

I turned around and smiled at Iuno. "You see, don't you?"

As seconds passed in silence, my smile fell.

"You're relying on the court to prevent war." Neither relish nor contempt marked his voice, only a quiet sadness. "But the last time they had a chance, they voted against peace. You did too."

Heat prickled my face. "It's different now," I said. "My father wants to lie. It's *base*. It lacks nobility."

"We're talking about a war." He stared at me. "Nobility has nothing to do with it. You need to look at the situation clearly, Ahpa."

I advanced from the window until I stood only a foot before him. "And what do you mean by that? The sun is almost down; the Great Circle won't happen today. You have no special vision, and you see no more clearly than me."

While I'd raised my voice, his remained level. "But I do. You're a prince of Hassam, and you believe in your House's virtue. You can't see its darkness. You can't see that you won't stop them."

My eyes widened. He truly was the same boy I had first met, a guest who had laughed in the face of a prince and, somehow, escaped punishment. Even as he dishonored the name of Hassam, I found that the lesser offense. "I *won't* stop them?" I curled my lip. "Now I understand. You want me to give up. You want me to be chained to the future, as you are."

"I only want you to accept the truth, Ahpa. The future holds war, and you can't change that."

"Stop *saying* that! When you speak your prophecies, do you enjoy reminding me of what I can't change? Surely it's amused you all these years, watching me fight for the smallest of chances to control my fate. Perhaps, instead of continuing to struggle in uncertainty, I really should live as you do, under destiny's unerring command. Just like a fucking slave!"

Then there was silence, except for a faint ringing as that scream—my scream —echoed off the walls.

Cold air rushed in from my bay windows, raising goosebumps on my arms. My full cup of tea still sat on the parlor room table. There was the bookcase where, on the top shelf, we stored our favorite collections of classical poetry, exchanged as gifts when we were boys. There was the mirror where I had tried to tame his curls with the palace's finest hair products, before giving up and suggesting he shave himself bald instead. There was the divan where we'd sat, side by side, and eaten dates.

"Iuno," I said.

"You have no idea." He was crying. "You've never seen."

I stood there, as anger washed out of me and shame rolled in. I could not remember seeing him shaken before, and now he stood before me, drowning.

"On Eshtan, I didn't always wake up with the day's knowledge. On the days when I did, I was useful. I told the village of a dust storm's approach, and we took shelter. I told the Samandirans that their military police would soon come for inspection, and they hid their Artani wives and children, so the police didn't whip anyone or take any children away. Whenever I saw a disaster approach, I also saw myself helping people. Saving people."

His tears guttered out. He turned his head to look out the bay window, as if his gaze crossed the distance between moons to look on his old home. "But I always liked the days when I didn't see the future better. On those days, whatever I did, I did it because I wanted to, not because I had seen myself do it. I was in control."

He looked up at me from the floor. I couldn't move.

"One day, the House of Hassam's hover-bombers came over the horizon. They hit the Samandiran garrison. I remember the screaming, the fire. Smoke everywhere. I didn't know that I would find *yima* and *yiba* under the rubble." He shook his head and smiled, even as I stepped backwards in shock. "I didn't see the future that day. I still believed that village boys controlled their own destinies. But since that day, I've understood—I have no power. Now, there isn't a morning that I don't see, because I'll obey whatever instructions destiny gives me, just like a slave, as you said. Why wouldn't I? I've nothing left to lose."

Words froze on my lips.

The smile slipped from Iuno's face. He stood, and I smelled my own shampoo on his hair as he brushed past me, and then he was gone, out the suite door.

The rain started again. I walked over to the bay windows and closed them, snuffing out the sounds of the city. Only the rain's pattering remained, fingers tapping on my skull, and I gave in under their weight, leaned against the wall, and fell to the floor. I did not know myself; I was no prince. I was that monster, screaming in rage at Iuno, ruled by my fear of the future.

Look at the situation clearly. I'd always thought myself so clever—I saw through the court's playacted nobility, the propaganda to glorify the House of Hassam. That messaging was for the commoners, not a prince. But I'd bought the same kind of lie as everyone else. Without thinking, I'd assumed that the enemy had killed Iuno's parents, because I didn't understand that a bomb was just a bomb.

I sat there for some time. The sunlamps began to dim, and as the hours passed, reality settled in my mind. Impending war with Samandir. The bleak chance that a Great Circle might prevent the slaughter. Iuno's revelation about his past.

He wasn't here, and I realized that even if Artan burned tomorrow, I needed to know that he was safe now. I stood, breathed, and left my suite.

I searched the common areas of the palace room by room. The few servants still awake cast each other nervous glances, wondering if they should offer help, wondering if I'd gone mad. I'd searched almost three full floors of the palace before I remembered—I was wasting my time looking indoors. I took the escalator down to the grounds and walked outside.

I had crossed half the courtyard before I realized that I had no umbrella, and rainwater was soaking my hair, weighing down the curls until they lost their definition, plastering them to my neck and back—

There he was, lying on the bench by the pond. Only the dim glow from palace windows above us illuminated him.

"I'm sorry," I said.

He tilted his head back to look at me. "You know, when I heard what you would say this morning, I wasn't surprised. I always knew what you thought."

"You knew me better than anyone else in the palace, then."

"You're good at hiding," he said, "but not that good."

I closed my eyes. "Please come inside. You'll catch cold out here. If you want the suite to yourself, I'll find a library for the night. If you want a different room entirely, I'll have it arranged. And if you want to stay here, I'll bring a tent."

"It's all right. I've slept in that suite with you for years. You're still the same person."

I stood there, turning his words over as the rain fell around me, and then I nodded. He took my offered hand to hoist himself off the bench, and together, we made it back to my suite. We toweled ourselves off in silence and stumbled into bed.

I was about to close my eyes when I realized what I'd forgotten to do. "The passphrase," I whispered to Iuno. "Clouds aflame. Flower verdigris. In a summer field, a single stone."

Then sleep took us.

I watched Iuno's face as he woke. I thought to capture the moment when the future's knowledge entered him. But he moved from sleep to wakefulness as easily as crossing a threshold, and his face betrayed neither surprise, nor dismay, nor understanding. His eyes merely slid open, and he turned to look at me.

"Ahpa," he said.

It was still me.

We dressed and ate breakfast together. I asked him about his childhood on Eshtan, and for the first time, he really talked. About the stories the soldiers told of life on Samandir, before they were conscripted. About the nights when he looked up and saw Artan, a blue disk crawling across the sky. About his parents. His *yima*, returning from the day's work, the smell of machine oil wafting off of her. His *yiba*, greeting her at the door with a kiss.

After we finished eating, I poured us two cups of tea. We nursed them on the divan.

"I have been an awful host to you," I said.

His eyes were closed; his nostrils dilated as he inhaled his tea's fragrance. "Yes. You have been."

"Though I have no right, I must ask you for something."

His breath whistled across his teacup's lip. "Go on."

"I will convene a Great Circle today. I will reveal what I know of the king's plan and do what is in my power to stop it."

My hands shook. Here, in the morning quiet, the world was still and ready to shatter at the lightest touch, a sheet of glass spiderwebbed with cracks. Tension pulsed in my temples, and sweat beaded my forehead. I didn't want to step forwards into the future. I couldn't look down.

The treasures and trophies of a prince's life surrounded me—my richly colored rug, the jeweled jacket hanging by my door, vials upon vials of hair cream and conditioner and gel. I exhaled and released it all. In my mind, the rain washed it down the hill to the river, and the waters took it.

"Please," I said, "come with me when I go. Watch what happens. So that you can tell me now, because you already see it, what happens in the Circle."

"And if I see that you fail..."

"Then you should tell me. I will still try. I must."

"You tell me," Iuno said, and I shivered at his words, "why you want it this way."

I leaned back into my divan and inhaled the scent, soaking its fibers, of home. Only darkness lay ahead of me.

"Because," I said. "Whatever happens, I won't hide from it."

Iuno says that we walk into the throne room together. He says—

The throne room is held, like a jewel in a scepter, in the palace's highest spire. As he walks inside, Iuno passes his eyes over the glass floors and walls, shining with reflected light. He can't believe it—we're so high up that we can watch the rainclouds roll over Artan's surface.

The princes, ministers, and generals watch us. The princes, my half-brothers, whisper among themselves. Iuno sees me in them—the curled black hair, the sharp, proud nose, and, in their eyes, the faint, ever-present glimmer of fear. Even in this glass room without shadow, their eyes dart from corner to corner, looking for hidden enemies.

King Azora Meira em-Hassam sits at the front of the room, his generals arrayed on either side of his throne. We kneel before him, and the room falls silent. Nobody knows why I have convened this Circle.

Iuno sees me trembling. After we leave the room, I will tell him that I wanted to run—that the knowledge that he gave me on the divan (that he gives me now, as he speaks) nearly strangled the words from me.

But still, I speak.

I address the princes and ministers in the room. I tell them of the king's plot to instigate another war with Samandir. For a moment, some of their faces break in shock, but they quickly conceal it.

I speak of honor and peace. How many of our bannermen will die in another war? How many Artani conscripts—merchants, students, engineers? How many of the enemy, sent to fight us by powers beyond their will, do we wish to kill?

All for a lie?

I place my resolution before them: the king must surrender his rule. Seconds pass in absolute silence.

Then the king breaks it. When he speaks, anger presses his words into a low growl.

First he turns to the ministers. *Remember,* he says, *when you bureaucrats and administrators feared that the enemy would destroy us? In the shadows, you whispered to me that I alone could save our House. You chose me as your king.* They avert their eyes and nod; half their number is gone.

Then he turns to his generals. *Remember,* he says, *when we took our army's leaders from the academy, not the battlefield? To replace them, I selected each of you regardless of your previous rank or station. I chose you for your strength, and together, we would have achieved total victory, were it not denied from us. Will you fight with me again?*

From the front, they roar their answer with one voice: *Glory to the king! Glory to the king!*

Then he turns to his sons. *Remember,* he says, *my generosity. War is my gift to you. Who among you will drive our armies into Samandir and attain greatness? Who will defend my legacy? I am still watching, and I have yet to make my choice.*

The princes glance at each other, and then they follow their father's eyes and look at me.

Softly, the king curses me. *You,* he says. *I thought you cunning and capable. To act, to war, to command—this is your province as a prince. What has rotted your mind?*

I do not answer him. Iuno understands: nothing remains to be said. I call for votes.

The outcome is obvious. The ministers think of themselves; if any of them vote with me but my motion fails, they're doomed. The generals want war, and they don't care how it comes about. And my brothers crave the power that my father dangles before them: a chance to rule fate instead of being ruled by it.

A minister counts the votes— unanimously, the Great Circle rejects my resolution.

Iuno stands next to me, silent. He watches as the king's hand rises.

I stood before my father in his throne room. Every word he'd spoken doubled in my ears; I heard, as one, the cold clarity of his voice as he spoke in the present, and the soft crackle of Iuno's voice as he relayed the king's words in the past. The uncontrollable tremor in my shoulders, the view of the clouds crawling beneath us —it was all as Iuno had said it would be. I, too, watched as the king raised his hand.

He extended his arm straight from his chest and curled his fingers into a fist, as if he grasped an invisible scepter. I exhaled. It was the Hassamite gesture of command.

"You no longer have power here," he said, "and you are nothing to me. If any power remained to you, I would command you to die—but now, you are beneath even that. So I command you instead to disappear. I will never hear you speak another word, and I will never see you again."

Cracks in his mask of royal calm revealed the contempt roiling beneath. As a child, I'd seen him as a great man. I had fantasized of sharing in his greatness. Now, I turned my back on him and let those fantasies fall from me. As Iuno and I walked out of the throne room, I looked straight ahead, without returning anyone's stare.

I had walked into the future knowing that I would not succeed. In that room, I had seen the great power of the wheels of war. Was my destiny to place my hands on them over and over, failing each time to stop their turning? Then I would do it, if only for the hope of one victory.

Our footsteps echoed in the narrow passageway as we descended the steps of the throne room's spire. My father had not ordered my execution, but he had killed whatever remained of Prince Meira Pashel em-Hassam in that room. A wild and roaring future now lay ahead of me. Perhaps it would carry me to distant lands and lives beyond my small imagination. Perhaps, in a week, it would dash me against the rocks.

We returned to our suite together. I waited until nightfall, when Iuno was asleep, to leave. In the note I tucked under his arm, I was not sentimental. I had forfeited that privilege when I called him a slave. Instead, I only left instructions on how to find an off-moon safehouse, beyond the reach of the House of Hassam and war, though I could make no guarantees.

I had already packed my bags that morning. I slung them over my shoulder, opened the bay windows, and leaned out. In a few minutes, I had rappelled down the palace wall and disappeared into the city.

If I had burdened Iuno with emotion in my note, what would I have said? In my head, I apologized to him for my endless offenses—the arrogance, the fear, the anger—that, frozen in the past, I could not erase. I wished him well as he walked into tomorrow, knowing that the future could not be commanded and hoping, as much as I could, all the same.

The herbal smell of tea bloomed in my nose; a fresh date's thick paste coated my tongue. It tore my heart, and I smiled. I thanked Iuno. It was fitting to remember him by this pain.

I'd made arrangements to leave the city by river ferry. The boat's silhouette, a black shadow punctured by light shining through the portholes, bobbed on the waves. The creaking of the wooden pier overlapped with the rush of water beneath me. One of my men waited for me by the entrance ramp to the boat.

He walked up. "Sir," he said, his voice low, "there's a problem."

I tensed. Not even out of the city, and already beset by obstacles. "What is it?"

"It's...him." By the dim starlight, I saw that he seemed more confused than frightened. "I don't know how he found the boat. Perhaps it's better if you speak to him directly."

And there he was, walking down the boat's ramp.

"Finding shortcuts down the hill has been useful," Iuno said. He yawned. "For things like this. Wherever we go next, I hope we won't have to live in one room for years on end. Maybe we can find some shortcuts together."

I only stared a moment before I burst into laughter. I didn't need to ask him how he'd found me. After a second, his laughter, exactly as ugly as I remembered, joined mine.

Eventually, the gravity of my situation reasserted itself, and the laughter died. "Iuno," I said, "this is foolish. There's too much danger in staying with me. And..."

We locked eyes.

Why would you want to?

"My time in the palace with you was interesting. Complicated," he said. "You were often cruel to me, without realizing it. But you were also kind."

His voice was soft. "I don't know what the future holds," he said, and at this, his lips twitched in an ironic smile. "You may become more cruel than kind, and then I'll slip away some night and walk alone. But I'm not ready for that yet. It's been some time since my life held something I cared not to lose."

I considered the qualities I wished for myself. For so long, I had striven to be nobler and bolder, but now I wanted to ride this boat to a place where I could find humility. Kindness. Where I could be happy to say that I was still myself.

I wanted to argue with Iuno and push him from my path, so that I knew, no matter what happened, I could harm him no more. But I had already harmed him, and here he remained. So, I only said, "Thank you."

"Besides," he said, holding up a lumpy bag, "you forgot your hair products."

"It's actually customary for exiled nobility to cut their hair. Perhaps I should do so before I board." I turned to my man, who snapped to attention. "Do you have a knife?"

Iuno's face crumpled into a pout of mock dismay. "Oh, let's not be so dramatic. That hair shouldn't go to waste."

I smiled.

After I boarded, we walked to the prow together. The boat cast off from the dock, and, gradually, the city's lights grew dimmer behind us. I closed my eyes and surrendered to the night.

See Albert Chu's story "When the Oracle Speaks" online at Metaphorosis.
If you liked it, leave a comment. Authors love that!
Remember to subscribe to our e-mail updates so you'll know when new stories are posted.

About the story

Future sight has been explored extensively in fiction. It's been around at least as long as classical mythology, with your Oedipuses of old failing to avoid the destinies set out for them by mysterious oracles. In contemporary times, we have Dr. Manhattan, seeing into the future with these poorly-explained tachyons, or time travelers from the future who come bearing news of apocalypses ruled by robot overlords. The idea for the story started out from a desire to explore future sight from a slightly different angle—what if, instead of these vaguely worded and cloudy prophecies, someone always knew exactly what was going to happen? They couldn't use this information to alter the future, because their vision is perfect;

what they see is what is going to happen. What kind of person would this be, and what sort of life would they live?

Various other bits of media I've consumed over the years got tossed into the ideation blender. The relationship between Iuno and Ahpa is reminiscent of how Madeline Miller writes Patroclus and Achilles in *The Song of Achilles*. The feudal space opera setting is taken straight from the pages of *Dune*—another work which also prominently features future sight. The thematic focus of the piece as an anti-war story came later in the brainstorming process. The concept of an unalterable future often evokes feelings of helplessness or a lack of agency—something so powerful that it's pointless to even think about trying to stop it. And I realized that such enormously powerful calamities, beyond the reach of any one person to stop, happen in the real world all the time. In the story, Ahpa finds himself in the same situation countless people have experienced in history—he knows war is coming, but there's nothing he can do about it.

Originally, I planned on making the viewpoint character Iuno himself. I was excited to write from the perspective of someone who already knows how the scene's going to play out—the entire first scene between Ahpa and Iuno was going to be Iuno seeing, in the future, their conversation, and then the scene would end with Ahpa actually walking into the courtyard. But the more I sketched the story out, the more I realized that, first of all, it was going to be quite difficult writing from the perspective of someone who is completely resigned to living his life out as a script, and second, the actually interesting character arc is, of course, Ahpa's. His story subverts some of the basic tropes of a hero, who's often expected to take action and change the situation. Ahpa starts out the story feeling entitled to those heroic privileges—he's a prince, after all, taking charge is his thing. So I structured things so I could end Ahpa's character arc with him having some greater understanding of surrender and a lack of power—while still putting a heroic twist on the story.

A question for the author

Q: Do you often include children in your stories? What role do they play?

A: Yes, and they're all teenagers—I have no idea how to write someone below the age of 13. I consumed some of the most impactful fiction to me when I myself was a teenager, and many of those stories featured characters my own age. I loved reading and watching stories about kids in colorful and fantastic settings, facing insurmountable odds, finding their inner hero—stuff that I'd consider a "guilty pleasure" nowadays, but it certainly left its mark. The teenagers in my stories are always heroes; I want them to be characters that I would have wanted to identify with.

About the author

Albert Chu writes speculative fiction out of Seattle, where he currently lives with his wife and a very energetic puppy. His writing transposes the ordinary concerns of his life into fantastic settings filled with lasers and magic. By day, he works as a mechanical engineer. His interests include anime, lifting weights, and PVP games with his wife.

albertchuwrites.com, @chubert_writes

The Princia Prologos

Aaron Zimmerman

Editor's Preface

The order of Gauntleteers requires its members to keep a journal of their experiences. The document you are about to read is such a journal.

Some consider these words fanciful fiction. Others take them as literally true. A group calling themselves the Church of Time has even adopted them as scripture.

While speculations abound, there are some things we do know:

A hunter discovered this text in the northern forest eight years after the events described therein, inexplicably preserved.

No gauntleteer has ever been able to manipulate time.

No one has ever found a river in the northern mountains.

No gauntleteer has ever managed to transport an object from one place to another instantaneously, let alone an entire army.

So what really happened?

I will not prejudice you with my own theories, but I will offer a counter-question: does it matter?

Maybe the value of a story comes more from the questions it asks than the provability of its events. And Miranda Southbrook, whether she means to or not, asks a most valuable question: what is more important, the present or the future?

And the answer? I will let her story speak for itself.

The Journal of Miranda Southbrook

The first day is for sickness
The second is for seeing
The third day brings us power
The fourth sets foes to fleeing
the fifth day is for making
On the sixth, we learn to fly
The seventh brings us wisdom
And on the eighth, we die

That was how my mother sang me to sleep. When I got older, I asked her if the song was true. She told me that one day she would put on the gauntlet, and for eight days she would be a living god, able to fix everything wrong with the world.

"And after eight days?"

"This is the thing about life, Miranda: it requires sacrifice."

I was thirteen when she ascended. I remember her far-away eyes. I cried and cried and begged her not to die. She found me a glass of water, patted me on the head, reminded me that life was about sacrifice, and then flew away.

I can't stop thinking about that song, even though my mother has been dead for years.

Her voice was not trained, it was more croak than croon, but I'd give nearly anything to hear it again.

Oh, gods, I can't believe I just wrote that. I was just kidding, I'm not actually some silly melodramatic child.

I need to start over.

My name is Miranda Southbrook. I am seventeen, a newly sworn initiate of the order of gauntleteers, on my first visit to the septum. I am the twenty-third in line to ascend, to claim the power of the gauntlet.

The first anointed, who is the next in line and leader of the order, gave me this journal an hour ago.

"No detail is too small," he said.

As gauntleteers cannot train with the object itself, for obvious reasons, reading past accounts is our best way to prepare.

It is tradition for new initiates to pass an hour alone reflecting in the septum after taking their vows, and here I am, staring at the gauntlet and not sure what to write about it. What would a future gauntleteer need to know that they haven't already read in the accounts of the gauntleteers before me?

But of course training isn't the only purpose of these journals. They are distributed widely and cherished by historians and minstrels. So really, this journal is my chance to tell my own story, to craft my legacy. Maybe I shouldn't admit such a thing, but my legacy is the reward for the sacrifices I've made along the way.

Asher asked me to go with him to the *Princia Prologos* tonight. It is a delightful play about a clever princess and a wicked queen. I dearly wanted to say yes, but here I am instead.

"The gauntlet's not going anywhere," Asher pouted.

He is a bit dramatic, my Asher. But I love that about him. He's indulgent and spontaneous and all the things I'm not. Perhaps that's why I agreed to marry him.

"There will be time for such things when I finish my training," I told him. And it's true: in a few years I will have all the freedom and means afforded to a fully trained gauntleteer. Unlike my mother, I won't let the order consume my whole life. I'll marry Asher and have a family and everything will be perfect. Years later, I will be called to ascend for the good of the kingdom, but there will plenty of time for plays and Asher before that happens.

And it's not just the gauntlet that keeps me from Asher's company. The Sagian prince is here, in our palace, to swear himself to our princess, and tonight there is a feast to celebrate the betrothal. The entire order will be there, sitting in a line from first anointed to newest novice, as we do for all occasions of state.

We have been fighting Sagia for generations, ever since they stole the other gauntlet, the right-handed one.

I sometimes think, as maybe all initiates do, that I could be the one to unite the gauntlets. I dream of the songs written in my honor, and the smile on people's lips when they say my name.

Miranda Southbrook, the hero whose sacrifice led to a better world for everyone.

But then, what if this nuptial-contrived peace holds?

What if there are no more wars?

I know I should want that. I know from the accounts how terrible war can be.

But my life bends toward the day I put on this gauntlet to perform deeds worthy of the greatest sacrifice of all.

And what could such deeds be, without a war? Shall I give my life to build bridges and mend walls?

Come and hear the ballad of Miranda and the great chimney cleaning?

No, when my times comes, far in the future, I will be a war-time gauntleteer. I will perform deeds worthy of the gauntlet and make my mother proud.

My visitation time expires. I have to dress for the feast. I feel like I wasted my time on wandering thoughts. I will ask for more time and focus on the gauntlet.

Everything is ruined.

I am alone in the sanctum, huddled by a brazier burning low without a chance of refilling.

I stare at the flames and shake my head, unable to move past the unfairness. But there is no changing it, and my obsession accomplishes nothing.

The betrothal was a trick. The Sagians came for the reason they always come: to steal the gauntlet. The king was blinded by his hubris, and now the princess is dead, and the city burns.

After the feast, I asked the first anointed for more time in the septum. He smiled indulgently, saying he remembered his own first night with the gauntlet and granting me another hour.

I hurried down the spiral stairs trying to shake the wine and music from my thoughts.

The door minder, Beatrice, opened the triple lock to the sanctum, let me in, and locked it behind me.

I was staring at the gauntlet, about to start writing a much different reflection than this, when I heard shouting outside the door.

I hurried to the door just as a soldier came running down the circular stairs.

"They've killed the princess," he said, his words all mushed up.

Beatrice turned back toward me immediately. She blinked once, her mouth straightening to a line.

"It is fortunate that you are here," Beatrice said through the locked door. "I honor your sacrifice."

She pulled a lever beside the door. Shells of solid iron dropped from above, sealing off the sanctum.

The last thing I saw was a Sagian soldier, garish in red and orange, stepping around the corner with a bloody sword in his hand.

And now Beatrice and the other guards must be dead or captured. The Sagian soldiers batter the iron shell. They are trying to get in. I don't think they know I am here.

And I have no food, no water, no hope.

I will die in here.

It has only just now occurred to me what Beatrice meant. "It is fortunate you are here," she said.

She meant the gauntlet. It is right there, grey in the fading firelight.

I can prevent Sagia from stealing it.

I can ascend.

It seems obvious in hindsight, yet I've only just now considered the idea.

Part of me thrills at the prospect of being the youngest gauntleteer ever, the savior of Redding, the hero of story and song.

But the price — I knew the day would come but it was always so far in the future it never really felt real. But here it is, eight days away and twenty years too soon. It is one thing to sacrifice yourself in the abstract 'eventually', but quite another to stare that sacrifice right in the leathery fingers.

It is such a tatty thing, like the face of a wicked queen in a play, wrinkles exaggerated to make sure all knew she was wicked.

I put off the gardens and the theatre for when I would have enough time. And now the time is gone. It is hard to believe. Eight days? I have eight days to live.

But I will die one way or another. I might as well prevent the Sagian bastards from stealing the gauntlet.

The constant clanging! It will drive me mad if it goes on much longer.

I will do it now.

I am the thirty-fourth gaunleteer.

There were no trumpets to celebrate, no speeches or ceremonial incense, unless you count the symphony of clanging hammers and chisels on the other side of the shell.

I could find no easy way to break the glass enclosure, so I toppled the whole pedestal. The glass shattered, scattering shards all the way to the wall ten feet away. I looked around, expecting someone to scold me for my disrespect, for my presumption.

I picked up the gauntlet and shook it free of glass. I only hesitated a moment before pulling it onto my left hand. It fit like it had been sewn for me.

The first day is for sickness, as the song goes. All I feel so far is a slight itch.

According to the accounts, there will be body pains, fever, unlike anything I've ever felt.

Morna Evensmith hated the smell of bread. Not the taste, but just the smell of bread baking. What a strange thing.

The itch spreads down my arm like crawling ants.

The fourth gaunleteer, Henry something or other, refused to read anything written down, saying he had trouble understanding words unless someone spoke them aloud. He paid people to read for him until his death.

Such trivial nonsense! I should be focusing on the sickness and its known abatements, and my traitor mind wanders to useless stories!

I cannot take the itching. It feels as if my whole body will shake free of its skin.

I wish I had gone to the play with Asher. The *Princia Prologos*. I wish I could hold his hand and kiss him, and he could tell me everything will be ok.

I think it's been about a day. It is hard to track the passing time. But the shaking itch recedes, so time must have passed.

I still can't believe this is happening: the peace shattered, a battle raging in the streets.

And down here, my life slowly ticks away to the sound of clanging chisels and banging hammers.

Day two is supposed to be for seeing, but I don't see anything. Well, actually, I can see this journal and the ghostly outlines of the sanctum. This must be through a manifestation of the power, as the brazier has long since burned out.

On day two, a gauntleteer must prepare her mind. That is what the accounts say. Day two is the calm quiet before the swell of day three.

But I'm just bored.

What if the power never comes, and I die down here, helpless and starving?

Only I'm not hungry. And there's the seeing without light. So the power must be real.

And my mother wouldn't have lied to me. There was no mistaking the power in her touch before she died.

Her eyes looked distant, sad. She wasn't really my mother anymore. She tried to be, offering me a glass of water as if that single gesture could compensate for years of absence.

I thought I would choose differently, that I would be a parent to my children. But here I am, turning into my mother after all.

By the time I noticed the power, it had been tickling the back of my awareness for a few hours.

"Our world is nothing but ideas and the will to bind them."

That is how Sathia Shoemaker described the feeling in her journal. That is how Will got its name.

The latent power feels like the ache that calls you to stretch after waking — or like the heaving of your belly when you hold your breath past comfort.

I laid my quill on the floor and tried to levitate it, using the trick of thought practiced in lessons: the quill is levitating, the quill is levitating.

And then it was. The feather hovered a few inches off the stone for a heartbeat and then fluttered back down.

I wept for a solid ten minutes. I don't know if it was relief, excitement, or despair. Probably all of them and more besides.

The power is real! I can move things with Will.

The power is real! I will be dead in a week.

I wiped my eyes and practiced. After an hour, it was as easy as breathing to spin the quill in circles and make it dart any which way.

I willed shards of glass from the gauntlet's case into the air and twirled them around each other like snow in a winter wind.

I took a break to record these thoughts.

But the power calls to me.

I am about to leave the sanctum. I am a day four gauntleteer and the power fills me like wine bulging the seams of a wineskin.

I practiced for hours and hours, feeling no fatigue. I think I will never sleep again. Or eat.

The Sagians are almost through the shell. In a moment, I will finish their work and peel back the metal like a curtain proclaiming the start of a story.

And then... I fight. I have never killed anyone before, and I keep imagining it. I am unsure if I will like or hate it, and both possibilities frighten me. I have a lot of fighting ahead. I wonder how long it will take me to rid the city of the Sagians.

I have no doubt I can do it. I am still mortal, but I can deflect an arrow or sword with no more than a thought. I can turn their weapons back upon them.

I try not to think about such things, but my imagination wanders to the future, to the songs written of the battle to come. I imagine the wide-eyed amazement when children hear the story of Miranda Southbrook from their parents over bowls of steaming porridge.

I chide myself for these childish daydreams, but without hope of a future, I can only fight for my legacy.

It is time.

I have done something much more terrible than killing. I have broken the world.

As planned, I peeled the shell away, revealing a half dozen grimy Sagians. They stared at me for a moment and then charged.

As planned, I obliterated them with a hail of metal and stone.

And then it was still.

I choked on my breath, sat, and wept for a few horrible minutes, reckoning with the horror of my actions.

I believe the gauntlet gives more than just control over objects. It connects its bearer to the world in a way no one has ever described. At least for me it does. My violence created — I don't know what — a wrongness, like a pillar of poison smoke disrupting a blue sky.

It seems to me now that all life is connected, part of a larger context, a meta-creature built from every living thing. Killing those soldiers was like cutting off my own hand. I don't mean to say I suffered more than they did. But the gauntlet connected me to this context in some way, and in the aftermath of my monstrous action, I could see the futility of violence with sudden, irrevocable certainty.

I saw only one way forward: I resolved never to kill again.

I was a day four gauntleteer. In my mother's song the fourth day 'sends foes to fleeing'. But I vowed instead to forswear violence entirely.

My nascent connection to the infinite life around me strengthened at my resolution, seeming to bloom in approval.

I marched up the stairs, daydreaming words of friendship.

A dozen more soldiers greeted me as I stepped into the palace. I started my speech, but they attacked before I'd spoken three words. One of them knocked over a pitcher of wine in his haste.

I parried, dodged, repelled, and screamed for them to listen!

But they would not. I was their enemy, and they would not stop.

"Just give me time," I yelled and pleaded.

They answered with slashes and spears and snickers. I deflected each without effort, but I was just one person, and as word spread, more and more of them joined the battle against me. I was still mortal. One mistake and I would be dead.

I wasn't going to convince them.

The blossoming connection to the life all around me turned to a thousand angry eyes and a thousand chiding voices. I felt like a girl again, disappointing my mother.

I deflected a sword, turned a spear, stopped an arrow. I didn't notice the dagger until it was flying by. It missed my head by inches.

I erupted in frustrated impatience.

I screamed for the soldiers to stop, just stop!

And they did.

They stopped moving entirely, along with everything and everyone else.

I keep replaying the moment, searching every detail for an explanation.

A soldier with a dented half-helmet and a mustache slashes toward me, his eyes bulging, his lips curling over yellow teeth. Over his shoulder, a red-haired woman points her elbow toward me, about to hurl another dagger. Beside her, a woman with a shaved head tightens the leather strap of her jerkin, turning toward me.

Beside the shaved-head woman is the wine-spilled table. The red runs in forked rivers to the edge of the table, swelling into droplets on the edge, preparing to fall.

But not falling.

Nothing has moved, not at all.

I think I have frozen time itself.

I don't understand how I did it or how I can undo it.

I have broken the world.

My mother did this to me. I am her experiment.

In search of an explanation, I searched the palace and the city for books, notes, anything.

I found the letter addressed to me in the drawer of my mother's study in the house I grew up in.

Miranda,

> *There is a river of Will high in the northern mountains. It runs off a cliff, spreading life and time to the corners of the world.*

> *My death approaches, but first, I have given you a cupful from this river to drink. If my theory is correct, it will give you power greater than any previous gauntleteer.*

> *Do not waste this gift. Use your time to the fullest. Make the world better, fix the problems no one else can.*
>
> *This is the thing about life, Miranda: it requires sacrifice.*
>
> *Sincerely,*
>
> *Celia*

She gave me liquid Will to drink! I remember the cup, remember drinking, remember the liquid tasting like water. But maybe my memory is colored with grief and anger. Maybe there was a strangeness to it.

Could such a drink have strengthened my power? Is that why I feel the connection, why I was able to stop time?

I feel like a child wielding a too-heavy battle ax.

How could she be so reckless?

I am angry and confused, and this constant stillness is breaking my mind.

I have uselessly tried yelling, "Continue!" and "Resume!"

I have wept and raged and broken things in petty insolence.

My mother did this, and I hate her for it, but I also miss her and wish she were here to hug me and tell me it will be okay.

I thought that perhaps there was some great injustice I needed to fix, and time would unfreeze like some child's tale.

So I set about righting wrongs.

I found every single Sagian within the palace and dragged their statue-bodies beyond the city walls. I swept the floors clean of their boots and threw their swords into the river.

When time resumes, it will seem to them as if they were transported in a single moment.

But my good deed did nothing for time.

I took to the city to find more wrongs to right. I mended a few roofs, and patched a few street cobbles. Nothing.

I found Asher at the fortifications just beyond the castle gates. I think he was to be part of a counter-offensive.

He is strapping on a leather jerkin. I imagine he has been saying things like, "I won't rest until I find her."

I tried to hug him, but it was like hugging a lifeless doll.

I think about the mountains to the north from time to time. I wonder if the river is real. In time, I may set out to find it.

I haven't written in a week.

Ha! A week. What would that mean? There is no sunset, no breakfast, no ablutions, no sleep. My eight-day countdown has been paused along with everything else.

When I feel the inclination, I lie down in my childhood bed in my mother's house. I stare at the overhead canopy, remembering dinners, Asher's touch, laughter.

When I can no longer stand it, I get up. And such I consider a day.

I haven't written because I don't have anything to write about. And why continue writing at all? There will never be another gauntleteer to benefit or a minstrel to compose a ballad.

But still, I feel called to explain, to justify. Maybe it is just naive hope.

I want to write the name 'Celia Southbrook' and circle it again and again. This is her fault. Her fault.

I sometimes see her, my mother, I mean, sitting in her chair with a book in her lap, tunelessly humming to herself.

She asks me what I am waiting for. She tells me I am wasting her gift.

I tell her how I took the sword away from a man about to stab another behind a fish-quarter tavern. I tell her about the coins I took from Shield Street mansions and gave to the poor.

My mother isn't impressed. She says I should keep searching. She says I'm missing the point.

And I tell her to piss off because she is a figment of my imagination.

It has been even longer this time. We could call it a month.

My reeling mind has started to fill in the stillness with motion, to give the frozen people speech and personality and desires.

Their conversation is just my mind's desperate attempt at normalcy. But I hear their voices, so how can I say for sure that they are not real?

There is Benedict, in a green doublet, just outside my house on his way to attend the *Princia Prologos*. He is impatient and grumpy, but in an endearing way. And talking to me always seems to cheer him.

Molly is half a block down the street in a lovely blue and gold gown, with one hand elegantly raised to shield her eyes from the sun. She is austere and elegant, maybe a bit snobbish. She thinks I am reckless and naive. I tell her I'm doing my best, but she never seems to believe me.

And there is Rickon! He is a boy of six or seven, crouched behind a door, about to leap out and scare a passerby. He never scares me, though. I am too wily. His antics always make me smile. Sometimes I bring him a treat, and his eyes widen, and he devours it as only a child can.

Perhaps they are not real, but they feel real to me, and they are all I have.

I visit Asher also, of course. But his voice is the hardest for me to conjure. He is too real in my memory to become imaginary.

I don't know how long it has been. I can no longer tell what is real.

I long ago ran out of things to write in this journal. But I cling to it like a raft in a storm. I trace over past entries with my finger, remembering a world with time in it.

But now I have something to write. I have decided to go north. I feel it tugging on me: my mother's gift, the river of Will. I have put it off because I will either find it or not find it, and both options frighten me.

I've just said goodbye to all of my friends. It was hard, but I must be strong.

Asher's goodbye was the worst of all. He told me he didn't want me to go. He told me that he was afraid I would die and never return.

I told him to be brave and wait for me. I kissed him and hurried away before I could change my mind. He stood still, strong, even though he wanted to chase after me, to beg me not to go.

I think about the *Princia Prologos* a lot — how I wish I could go back and go with him.

The river is dry.

It took an eternity of searching. But I have plenty of time!

I finally found it nestled between two peaks high in the mountains.

The riverbed runs off a cliff, from which Will should fall and spread like morning mist.

But the river is dry.

I followed the riverbed to find the source, thinking maybe it was blocked.

I walked and walked, and somehow I never left the same valley, never escaped the shadow of those two peaks.

This is a special place — a place that doesn't work like other places.

My search was for nothing. I had thought that I could restart time by finding the source of Will. But it was for nothing.

I have explored every inch of this river bed many times over. There is nothing to be done here.

I will return to Redding soon. At least there, I have statue-friends.

Here it is just me.

But there is something about this place. Life is here — a river of Will, passing in a constant current. Or at least it *should* be here.

It is a good place to write stories. I write them on thick, rough papyrus — tales of wicked queens and daring adventures.

Just now, I wrote a story about a tree that kept growing through storms and fires and chopping axes.

The story unlocked an impossible bit of hope.

It is foolish and vain beyond belief, but I still dream of songs.

I sometimes lie down with this journal in my arms, cradled like the child I will never have. It is my only source of hope.

I know what I have to do. The answer has been in front of me all this time. But I couldn't see it. I didn't want to see it.

It came, as perhaps all realizations do, from stories.

At first, I wrote stories as a diversion. But soon, I wrote because it was the only way I could survive. I wrote to inhabit a world that made sense.

I wrote of imaginary people and places, but also, I wrote a story about when

Miranda said yes when Asher asked her to go to the *Princia Prologos*. I wrote a story about when Miranda told her mother she didn't want to be a gauntleteer but rather mix herbs into potions in a cottage far away from Redding. I wrote about the many lives I could have had.

Along the way, a realization snuck into my words, waiting for me to find the courage to notice it.

It is my fault. Not my mother's.

I stopped everything because the world would not listen to me. I used my untrained power like a naive child to get the one thing I thought I needed: time.

And now I hold it fast because my secret self clings to stasis.

It is what I always wanted: a chance to sacrifice for the future, to solve every problem there is or will be. I can fix the social inequities, heal the sick, and design a fair system of government. With infinite time, I could accomplish infinite things. And all it costs is my infinite loneliness.

It is an absurd belief. I know that. But I cling to it anyway. And why? I don't have a clear reason. I suppose I am afraid.

I have tried to overpower my subconscious hold on time with shouted declarations and quiet whispers, all in vain.

You cannot lie to yourself, not really.

But I think I have a solution.

There is one thing in my life that binds me to the future, to my sacrifice-strewn legacy.

One thing nurtures my hubris.

One thing that I could give up, if and only if, I genuinely wanted my present to resume at the cost of my future.

This journal.

This journal is the story of myself, told for the benefit of the future.

This journal is proof of my continued choice to sacrifice my present for my future.

I have to give that up, irrevocably and wholeheartedly.

And I will. I will.

I will throw you off the cliff and watch you flutter and fall like a bird without wings.

It will work. I am sure of it.

The wind will stir my hair, and I will turn to see the river rushing toward me.

And then I will be a day four gauntleteer again. My power will start to grow until it consumes me. My life will be finite. What a thing! What a wonder!

On day six we learn to fly. Where might I go? Day seven brings wisdom, but I think I have found that already.

I don't know what I will do with my four days. But even if I did know, I wouldn't write it here. Because I don't need to anymore. I don't care what you think of me, imaginary composer of ballads. You are not my life. You are a lie I told to myself to justify sacrificing every bit of today for tomorrow.

This world will change and change regardless of my little life, and eventually, you will forget even my greatest deed.

What wonders will I miss along the way?

The smell of candied nuts and sour beer.

The calm that settles the trees before a rainstorm.

Asher's hand in mine.

I could agonize about the wasted time, but that would only waste more.

I will have four days. What a gift!

Four days of breathing, of kisses and sunsets.

I would throw away a thousand eponymous ballads for that chance.

Goodbye, my dear, flawed future.

This is the thing about life, Miranda: it is happening now.

Editor's Epilogue

Miranda Southbrook was unquestionably in the septum during Sagia's failed attempt to steal the gauntlet.

The palace was unquestionably cleared of Sagian soldiers in what felt like a moment to all witnesses.

Four days after that sudden victory, the septum was discovered fully restored, with the gauntlet back in its place.

Miranda Southbrook's whereabouts and deeds during those four days remain uncertain.

Many claimed to have seen her in passing or even that she offered some service to them. From such stories, the phrase 'must have been Miranda' emerged as a verbal shrug to an unexplained turn of good luck.

My favorite story, though, is of a young woman matching Miranda's description attending the final performance of the

Princia Prologos three days after the Sagian retreat.

I imagine her in the third row, her eyes rapt with attention. She weeps and laughs and cheers at all the right moments.

She feels the wind in her hair and snuggles into her companion's shoulder, content and very much alive.

See Aaron Zimmerman's story "The Princia Prologos" online at Metaphorosis.
If you liked it, leave a comment. Authors love that!
Remember to subscribe to our e-mail updates so you'll know when new stories are posted.

About the story

When I get an idea for a story, I add it to a list in my phone's reminders app. The reminder I wrote for this story (probably while running) was, "There is a glove that gives almost unlimited power for seven days and then burns out the body of its wearer". Often ideas sit on that list for months or forever (There are currently 354 such pending ideas), but that one kept popping back into my thoughts, and I almost immediately began writing it. It took a bit of experimenting to find the now-obvious protagonist for such a premise: a young person forced to choose to end their life tragically early to use the power for some greater good. In early drafts, the story followed a linear build of Miranda's power, while at the same time, Miranda grew more and more disappointed with her inability to convince people to stop killing each other. My wife said, "It sounds like a meditation on how you feel like the world doesn't understand you". And she was right. It was a compelling idea, but not really a story. I went back to it and found a better story in Miranda's desperation: a story about the versions of ourselves we are so sure we have to live up to while there are lives unlived just beyond our ability even to see, let alone pursue.

A question for the author

Q: Have you ever wondered whether ideas are thought waves directed at you by an AI supercomputer located in the distant future?

A: In a way, yes. I think a lot about (and my story actually ruminates a bit on) life contexts. Specifically, I think there is a life context that we, as humans, can't directly interact with. It is a context that combines all humans (and other animals) into a meta-life structure with its own motivations, language, and consciousness. It is similar to how human bodies are made up of living cells. In both cases, the components live their lives, many fulfilling a purpose, and then they die without impacting the existence of the higher-order life. This "Sum of all Life" is far beyond our ability, as its constituents, to comprehend. But I think our ideas for stories, inventions, etc, are likely influenced by it. It isn't exactly artificial, but it is certainly foreign (some might call it divine.) And it likely exists within a different understanding of time, so we might call it the future. It needs things from us the way we need things from our white blood cells. And stories are likely a large part of that influence. Look, you humans, it says, I need more of you to start living for the present instead of the future, and out comes a story to try to spread that message.

About the author

Aaron is a writer, software engineer, and musician. When not daydreaming up stories, Aaron can usually be found conducting musicals in the western Chicago suburbs. Love to Katy, Elijah, Oliver, and Arthur.

aarontellsstories.com, @apzimmerman

The Antidote for Longing

Karl Dandenell

Part 1

The soldiers made no secret of their arrival; far from it. The lead pair of riders galloped into the outer courtyard below, scattering the peacocks, who set up a furious and discordant song of complaint. They redoubled their efforts several minutes later when the carriage and rear guard arrived.

I hated the peacocks. Loud, ridiculous creatures. However, they were already established on the grounds when I acquired the house, and my clientele loved them, so they stayed. It was all part of my façade: Lars Bjornsen, courtier and former advisor to Emperor Gustavus Adolphus, retired from imperial service and living a quiet life as an importer of fine victuals. My connections at court—real or perceived—set me apart from other merchants. Beneath this façade lay resentment and worry, for an exile from the imperial court is never truly safe.

I'd been dreading this moment for three years, ever since my dearest friend Fredrik Magnusson, the imperial physik, had hurried me into a carriage in the middle of the night with nothing but a hastily packed bag. "Don't blame yourself," he'd said. "There's no way you could have known the tsar's son was delayed."

"But I should have known something was wrong. Aleksey Mikhaylovich is never late for anything."

The timing of my plan had relied on Aleksey's punctuality and secrecy. I knew his servants followed strict orders to prepare the remote cottage with fresh food and bedding, then vacate the area. I also knew I had a brief window, perhaps half an hour, to add a fresh batch of Miner's Fate to the brandy before Aleksey's current mistress arrived. Miner's Fate was favored by the Soldiers of Night, an anti-Tsarist sect.

"Irina always gave him the honor of the first toast. Always," I said. "The reports were very clear on that."

"Alas, people are not as predictable as machine mage devices," Fredrik said. "What can one do?"

I'd hunkered beneath a nearby bush, visualizing the scenario. When Irina arrived, she would lay out their meal. Aleksey would ride in soon after, and the couple would dine. The poison would take hold gradually, bringing on a gentle melancholy and heaviness of limbs.

When I was sure both of them were dead, I was to leave a letter from the Soldiers of Night claiming responsibility.

But Irina had apparently grown tired of waiting. I'd watched in frustration and fear as she sat on the cabin's step, wrapped in a blanket, drinking a large snifter of brandy.

"I could have acted," I said. "Could have given her the antidote and said I was part of the tsar's secret guard. Something."

"Perhaps. We'll never know."

"No, we won't." By the time I'd gathered my wits together, Aleksey had arrived. It was all I could do to elude capture and make my way back to Stockholm.

"Banishments aren't forever. You'll be fine."

"You're an excellent physik but a terrible liar, Fredrik."

Rather than deny it, he'd clapped me on the shoulder and ordered the driver to make haste.

That was the last time I saw Stockholm.

Now, I barred the door to the solarium and unbuttoned the secret pocket of my waistcoat. Hidden within was a tiny silver flask given to me when I completed my training with the Society of Poisoners.

I kept the flask filled with *Dream Caller*. One good swallow would painlessly stop my heart.

Dream Caller is one of the first compounds taught to poisoners. It has to be ingested, unlike *Angry Falcon*, which is delivered by knife point, so the compound presents less danger to the student. The last time I'd administered *Dream Caller* was four years ago at a Midsummer gala, when Duke Emil had drunkenly referred to the emperor as 'Gustavus the Last'. His bowl of chanterelle soup was the perfect medium: the white pepper masked the *Dream Caller*'s slightly astringent aftertaste, and the broth's warmth improved its absorption.

Duke Emil's death unfolded so quietly everyone thought he'd merely fallen asleep between courses. Just another old man who'd had too much wine.

I added hot water to my teapot, stirring in a handful of leaves from yesterday's delivery: smoked black tea with dried orange peels from Iberia. As the tisane's perfume permeated the room, I reviewed my desk. Just correspondence with distant cousins and invoices. Nothing incriminating, nor particularly interesting: an accurate measure of my life in exile. I would leave behind no spouse or children. No lover would mourn my passing. Ironically, I was the perfect target for an assassination.

I poured myself tea and added half the flask to the cup. The tea was too hot to gulp, so I gave myself a moment. No sense in rushing into the afterlife with a burned tongue. Besides, the oak door was good and stout, made as it was from the timbers of a decommissioned imperial warship. It had held off French cannons; it would hold against fists quite easily.

However, no such pounding ensued. All I heard was a gentle knock and the faint voice of my old seneschal, Pontus.

"General Bjornsen?" he said.

"What is it?" I called loudly, mindful of his poor hearing. Pontus had served in the artillery squads in Iceland.

"A messenger wishes entrance."

I rubbed the condensation from the nearest window. The carriage lacked horses or even harness points. Instead, it was powered by two large, expensive demon jars connected to the front and rear axles. Few in Järna could afford such spellcraft, and they were all gentry. Hardly the sort of people to arrive unannounced.

But then I saw the purple *vimpel* hanging from the carriage's front post. Clearly the visitor was not just a messenger, but someone on imperial business.

"Praise Saint Catherine." I made the sign of the cross, a habit from childhood. Then I dumped the tea into the fire and returned the flask to my waistcoat.

If someone wanted me dead, they wouldn't bother with such theater. Far easier to hire a sniper to put a musket ball through my window, or a knife in my kidney at the marketplace. "It appears I'll live another day," I said.

"What was that, sir?"

"Bring them up!" Hope infused my voice. The appearance of an imperial messenger after all this time might—just might—indicate that Emperor Gustavus Adolphus had forgiven my transgression, or at least forgotten it. The passage of years both tempers our bile and dulls our memory, and the emperor was nearly seventy.

"Yes, sir."

"And Pontus—see that their escort is given some mulled wine." I recalled my own time riding winter escort duty. It was both honor and challenge. You spent hours in the saddle, hunched against the cold, straining your ears for the sudden explosion of hoofbeats behind you. A warm cup at your destination was a gift from heaven.

"Lt. Birgitta Pernillasdotter, my lord," said the imperial messenger with a precise court bow. "At your service." She was young for such a posting, perhaps twenty.

Her formal uniform consisted of black boots, trousers, blouse, and a tight-fitting coat with cuffs and collar trimmed with white fox fur. Her hat was bare except for a single ostrich plume. Rather than a court sword, she carried a gold-chased flintlock on one hip and a ceremonial dagger—suitable for cutting wax seals—on the other.

A quarter century ago, I had carried a more functional blade in my boot, its sheath painted with rose buds, one for every Prussian sentry I'd killed on moonless nights. It is strange, the things we take pride in.

"Welcome to Järna, Lieutenant. Be at ease," I said, responding with a salute as smooth and automatic as breathing. "It's just General Bjornsen, now. Retired." I straightened the lapels of my silk manteau and pointed to a chair. "Now, what brings you to my home?"

"The imperial physik sends his compliments," she said, handing over a packet of creamy white paper sealed with violet wax. "And requests you accompany me."

I hesitated over the seal. "Am I to understand this wasn't sent by the emperor?"

"No, sir. I would have said so."

Then it isn't a pardon. "I accept the message, Lieutenant." I tucked away my disappointment and opened the packet.

My dear friend,

> *Gustavus Adolphus is quite ill and I need your assistance. Please come at once.*
>
> *—Fredrik Magnusson*
>
> *P.S. I have shared your situation with Lt. Pernillasdotter. She is both clever and discreet.*

Though I recognized Fredrik's exquisite quill work and his favorite cobalt blue ink, the nature of the message struck me as uncharacteristically pithy. Normally his letters ran to several pages. During our days at the Imperial Academy, he loved to fatten his prose with lines of poetry or quotations from Marcus Aurelius. I admit I often spurred him on, especially after a glass or three of cheap brandy.

His brevity now was both plain message and subtle warning about the messenger. *Clever and discreet* was a phrase we used to describe soldiers we suspected of being enemy spies. "Alas," I said. "I am no longer welcome in the capital." Fredrik of all people knew this.

Birgitta informed me the imperial family was not in Stockholm. Rather, they were touring the provinces as part of Gustavus Adolphus's extended birthday celebration. "The emperor and empress are presently guests at Strömsholm Palace, a few hours away. Once the escort's horses are given a brief rest and watered, we can return at good pace. The carriage's demon jars are fresh," she added.

I was relieved. Hiring a machine mage to charge those jars would be ruinously expensive, even if we could find one on such short notice. Järna didn't attract many mages, given the nearest demon factory was a full day's ride away.

I re-read Fredrik's note. Together, we had faced cannon fire and treated our fellow soldiers in bloody field hospitals throughout Europe. In fact, it was Fredrik who'd pleaded with Spymaster Maja Viklund to show mercy, even though my error had almost plunged us into war with Russia.

I sometimes flattered myself that Maja had spared my life because we had once been lovers as devoted to each other as we were to our callings. More likely, though, Fredrik's intercession had simply provided her with sufficient political rationale to stay her hand. Having me executed outright might have raised the ire of the Society of Poisoners.

As far as Fredrik's request was concerned, honor and duty demanded I support the emperor any way I could. Beyond that, I wanted to help Fredrik, for he was the closest thing I had to a brother. Not seeing him these past few years had been one of the most difficult challenges of my exile. "Give me an hour," I told her. "The servants will provide a light meal in the sitting room."

I exchanged my silk clothes for my old field uniform and great coat. Then I shaved off my oiled and perfumed beard, leaving behind a mustache trimmed in the traditional cavalry style. While Pontus put a final polish to my old boots, I secreted several items about my person, including a poniard and a fresh vial of *Dream Caller*. Should this errand go badly, I had no intention of facing the noose.

Thus outfitted, I boarded the carriage after Birgitta, looking every inch the retired officer and not at all a disgraced poisoner.

We rolled away from the peacocks and their complaints.

I tucked a thick embroidered wool and silk blanket around my legs and pulled my plain beaver cap over my ears. Though residual heat from the demon jars leaked into the carriage, winter still gripped my bones. The sun might as well be the moon, for all the warmth it produced. Pontus, an Iceland native, would consider this fine weather. "Tell me, Lieutenant," I said, "what do you think troubles His Imperial Majesty?"

"He suffers from gout and dyspepsia, according to Lord Fredrik," said Birgitta. "The servants have strict orders not to agitate the emperor. Even the musicians are silent, lest they interrupt his rest."

"You don't sound very convinced."

"The stable master is an old friend. He found it odd that the emperor was riding every day without complaint, then suddenly required bed rest as if he were a woman swollen with child."

"Without casting aspersion on the imperial physik, I will acknowledge that he can be quite cautious when it comes to his patient's health," I said. "I'm sure he has matters well in hand."

"And yet here you are, summoned back to court on short notice," said the messenger.

"Lord Fredrik is also an old friend," I said, somewhat testily. "And as such, he has *asked* me to visit and offer what small wisdom I might have regarding His Imperial Majesty's illness."

She inclined her head. "My apologies, General. I meant no offense."

"None taken."

"However, given your former role at court, one can only speculate that matters are more serious than they appear."

Oh, she was a sly one, this messenger. She demonstrated all the hallmarks of one schooled in the imperial court's intrigue. A feint here, a retreat there. Nothing too direct.

I leaned forward and lowered my voice. "Lord Fredrik says you are discreet."

"Discretion is a necessary quality in a messenger, even more so when one serves the imperial family."

"Then I encourage you to exercise that discretion. Am I understood, Lieutenant?"

"Perfectly, sir."

I nodded and sat back against the leather bench. As the miles passed, we settled into silent contemplation of the scenery. At this time of year, the road was nothing but gray stones bordered by gray trees, their branches bare. Even the occasional bird was a welcome respite from the monotonous landscape. As we bumped along, I reviewed Birgitta's news in the context of the larger picture. If I were still at court (if only!) and Fredrik told me the emperor was 'quite ill', I would be closeted away with advisors, preparing for the worst. Especially given that the imperial family was currently far from the relative safety of Stockholm.

Two years before, the emperor's only child and heir, Gustavus Adolphus II, had drowned while crossing Lake Vatten in April. The winter had been unusually warm, leaving behind thinner ice than normal. That summer, when typhus took the empress to her own heavenly reward, there wasn't a church or town square that lacked for mourners. The country was devastated. Ambassadors from across the empire appeared, laden with letters proclaiming their condolences while offering prayers and—according to gossip—offers of marriage.

Once the formal grieving period had passed, the emperor moved quickly to arrange his betrothal to Anna Schlüssen of Prussia, a young, widowed noblewoman known for her archery and fierce chess game. She had also previously birthed two healthy boys, a testament to her fecundity.

Unfortunately, the new empress had failed to produce an heir with Gustavus Adolphus.

If he died now, there was no clear succession. The emperor had—wisely or not—chosen to appease the royals by blocking his stepsons from the throne. That left eight cousins with questionable claims, most of whom had been quietly raising mercenary levies since the old empress' funeral. If it came to civil war, the empire would surely shatter like a rotten log struck by a cannonball. Our enemies would invade, and Stockholm would burn. I shuddered to think of it.

One of the lead riders shouted a warning. I pushed open the window to get a better look just as his horse stumbled and pitched forward.

Above us, the driver yelled, "On the left! Black ice!" He engaged the brake, but not too hard, lest the wheels lock and we slide off the road completely. The heavy carriage crunched the thin layer of nearly invisible ice, coming to a stop a hundred paces later. Birgitta opened her door and freed her pistol.

"Stay here," she said and stepped down lightly, testing the ground. Her head swiveled back and forth as she scanned the forest. The other lead rider, a woman with a long braid tucked into her coat, circled back to take up position close to the carriage. She readied a musket.

I leaned out the open door. The fallen horse lay on the ground, its rear legs kicking weakly. Birgitta was helping the escort to his feet. The remaining riders made slow circles, weapons held ready. Their horses' breath steamed.

"Damn shame," said the driver. "Helvig's only had that mount for a fortnight."

"He seems all right," I said, watching Helvig crane his neck and slap his chest holster and sword belt. I felt that instinct in my gut: after you were thrown from your mount, the first thing was to check yourself and your weapons. Were you wounded? Could you fight?

"Aye, he's a tough lad. Eat a bowl of *surströmming* for breakfast and cut down trees until sunset," said the driver.

"Just stay upwind of him," added the rider.

Birgitta offered Helvig her pistol. He shook his head and readied his own weapon. Very slowly, he knelt and put his hand over the horse's eyes. I couldn't hear him, but I suspect he was whispering to it. Then he pulled the trigger. The report echoed loudly in the relative silence. He and the messenger then holstered their weapons and began unstrapping his saddlebags. In a few minutes, they had stowed everything inside the carriage's lockbox. Helvig took his musket and climbed up next to the driver. Birgitta returned to her spot on the bench inside and thumped the ceiling.

"Make for Rönninge depot!"

"Aye, ma'am!" He unlocked the wheels and we slowly picked up speed.

She said to me, "We'll pick up a fresh mount for Helvig and get you to Strömsholm without further delay."

"How is Helvig?" I asked.

"His backside will be black and blue tomorrow, but nothing a bowl of ale won't fix."

Soon we spied the depot. It was a small place, mostly ancient low stone walls with a newer wooden outer wall. Its *vimpel* barely stirred in the light breeze. Birgitta stepped out as soon as we came to a stop and strode up to a soldier stacking firewood. "What's your name?"

"Private Lundson, ma'am." He dropped the firewood and gave a sloppy salute.

"I'm Lt. Pernillasdotter. Tell your commander we need your freshest horse saddled on the double. We lost one about a half hour down the road to black ice."

"Ma'am. Yes, ma'am!" he said and jogged off. I exited the carriage and casually stretched my legs, trying to work some stiffness out. I observed a pair of sentries at the gate and another walking along the outer wall. Between them they had clear firing lines covering the road in both directions, although they didn't seem particularly alert.

Private Lundson returned in the company of another man, a young captain with dueling scars on one cheek. His flat cap sported a white feather and a jaunty red ribbon. A gift from an admirer, perhaps.

"Hallo!" said the officer. "Sorry to hear about the loss of your animal, but I just can't give you a horse and tack without proper requisition. There has to be an accounting for everything that leaves the outpost."

Birgitta smiled. "Captain...?"

"Nyberg."

"Captain Nyberg—let me remind you that everything in this depot, down to your wool socks, belongs to the emperor. It would be a shame if I had to report that I was delayed because some prissy officer wouldn't give us a fresh mount."

Nyberg put a hand on his sword. "Are you threatening a superior officer?"

"No one is threatening anyone," I said, stepping forward. "However, as much as I admire your dedication to procedure, *Captain*, we have important business that cannot be delayed." I checked my pocket watch. "We're leaving in five minutes."

Nyberg narrowed his eyes, his posture tense. I could see he was considering and discarding his options. As much as he thought he could push around a junior officer, he had no such leverage with me. He'd have to make this a challenge of honor and settle it with steel. After taking my measure, he snapped an order at Lundson, who took off running even faster than before.

"Anything else, sir?" he asked.

"No, Captain. You have the emperor's gratitude."

He saluted. Birgitta said, "You might want to send a squad down the road to collect the corpse before it draws wolves. At the very least, collect the saddle."

Nyberg nodded and trod away with quick, heavy steps.

Five minutes later, Lundson reappeared with a great beast of a black horse, saddled and ready. "This is Baldur, Captain Nyberg's horse. He was getting ready to ride patrol when you showed up." He handed the reins to Birgitta, who passed them to Helvig.

"My compliments to the captain," said Helvig, offering up his hand for the horse to sniff. "I'll take good care of him."

"Anything else, ma'am?"

Birgitta shook her head. "Dismissed."

We resumed our journey. Once we'd made up some time, Birgitta seemed to relax. She drank from a leather water skin and passed it to me.

"Permission to speak frankly, sir."

"Of course." I gulped water as we bounced over a rough patch.

"Would you mind telling me why you intervened back there?"

"I don't like bullies," I said. "And Nyberg is a bully, which is probably why he's commanding a supply depot in the middle of nowhere rather than Stockholm or Göteborg."

"I see." She nodded. "So that wasn't some misplaced display of chivalry?"

She wasn't completely wrong. When I was in the field, few women served in her capacity. "If it was, it was unintentional, Lieutenant." I returned the waterskin. "I'd wager a gold crown you could soundly thrash the captain. If it came to that."

"If it came to that, you'd win," she said with a wicked grin.

The ride became markedly smoother once we attained the main supply route between Malmö and Stockholm. It had originally been laid out by Romans and improved upon and extended by Swedish engineers ever since. It was common in summertime to encounter gangs of political prisoners doing road repair in exchange for reduced sentences.

In another hour, we saw signs for Västerås, which put us close to Strömsholm Palace. The driver rang a warning bell and eased off the brakes, increasing our speed. The outriders spurred their mounts to keep up. Fortunately for the horses, we reached the castle soon enough.

Strömsholm was a cold, dismal place in winter, its gardens nothing but ice-frosted bare bushes, its lake empty of boats. Even the swans had the good sense to be elsewhere.

The driver delivered us through a small gate far from the main entrance while our escort peeled off toward the stables. As the gate closed behind us, I kept an eye on the messenger's hand resting near her pistol. I didn't believe she would arrest me now, but there might be others outside, soldiers with different orders. With careful movements, I loosened my blanket. Should events go amiss I might be able to fling it over her and wrest the pistol away. A lifetime of wariness breeds such thoughts.

We rolled to a stop and the door was opened from without. No jailers waited with irons. Birgitta saluted and leaned back so that I might exit first as senior officer.

With great relief, I returned her salute, grateful for this small courtesy. As my first commander liked to say, anyone can purchase court privileges, but military perquisites are earned.

I winced as I stepped onto the flagstones. Even this well-maintained carriage was a challenge to my knees. All that time in the saddle and too many winter campaigns had taken their toll.

Out of habit, I glanced up at the main tower's flagpole. The rectangular sun and ocean banner snapped in the cold breeze, indicating the presence of the imperial family. And their attendants, including the imperial physik and spymaster, neither of whom I'd seen since Stockholm.

A wave of nostalgia and pride washed over me, quickly followed by a deep sorrow. It was one thing to don the uniform and transform myself into a soldier, but the imperial court was an entirely different, more dangerous battlefield. My heart ached to be part of it once again.

Despite my banishment, I had arrived safely. Perhaps my luck was improving.

See part I of Karl Dandenell's story "The Antidote for Longing" online at Metaphorosis. If you liked it, leave a comment. Authors love that!
Remember to subscribe to our e-mail updates so you'll know when new stories are posted.

About the story

"The Antidote for Longing" isn't my first story set in an alternate 17th Century Sweden. Before this, I wrote several shorter pieces, including "The Machine Mage of Umea", which explores the demon-powered technology that helped create the Scandinavian empire (think steampunk but with supernatural beings).

My own family traces its roots to Sweden, and further back to Belgium (to the region of Andenelle). There, the Dandenell clan was well known for their impressive silver and iron creations. In fact, they worked on the gates at Versailles.

The story goes that the Swedish king, upon touring Versailles, was so taken with the ironwork that he hired my great-great-etc. grandfather Clas Dandenell (along with various relations) and moved them to

Sweden so they could help with the gates at Drottningholm Palace.

At the time, the Swedish military did not have cannons as powerful or accurate as, say, the French. My ancestors helped correct that. So it may be that the Dandenell design esthetic was less valuable than their skill fabricating artillery.

When I sat down to write "Antidote", I wasn't looking to write an action-based military story; I was more interested in the characters who had served a military empire and the personal costs of such service. Plus, I wanted to play around with the idea of court assassins, specifically poisoners. (My interest in poisons was probably inspired by an organic chemistry class in college, well before I abandoned the sciences for the more genteel academic path of Shakespeare, Milton, and Chaucer.)

Finally, I saw the main character, Lars Bjornsen, as something of a contradiction. He was both a military commander and an assassin, representing the open and secret faces of the empire. When he was banished, it forced him to question his past and future. That sounded like an interesting vein to mine.

A question for the author

Q: Do you prefer your SFF as books or movies?

A: That's a tough question. I've always been a big fan of SFF movies. As a kid, I loved the low-budget British stuff and Japanese kaiju films. However, once I joined the Science Fiction Book Club—with its dubiously copy-edited editions and cheesy covers—I was hooked on the printed format. From my early days as a fast-food scullion to my most recent corporate gig, I've always kept a paperback or e-reader in my backpack so I could cram in a chapter or two at lunch. These days, I get more of my fiction from podcasts (which are great for house chores and weeding the yard), but at the end of the day there is something special about curling up with a cat and book.

About the author

Karl Dandenell is a graduate of Viable Paradise and a Full Member of the Science Fiction & Fantasy Writers Association. He and his family, plus their cat overlords, live on an island near San Francisco famous for its Victorian architecture and low speed limits. His preferred drinks are strong Swedish tea and single malt whiskey. This is Karl's third appearance in *Metaphorosis*, following "Comes the Tinker" and "Papa Pedro's Children."

www.firewombats.com, @kdandenell

Copyright

Title information

Metaphorosis July 2023

ISSN: 2573-136X (online)
ISBN: 978-1-64076-261-9 (e-book)
ISBN: 978-1-64076-262-6 (paperback)

Publisher

Metaphorosis

a magazine of speculative fiction

Metaphorosis Magazine is an imprint of
Metaphorosis Publishing
Neskowin, OR, USA

www.metaphorosis.com

"Metaphorosis" is a registered trademark.

Discounts available

Substantial discounts are available for educational institutions, including writing workshops. Discounts are also available for quantity purchases. For details, contact Metaphorosis at metaphorosis.com/about

Metaphorosis Publishing

Metaphorosis offers beautifully written science fiction and fantasy. Our imprints include:

Metaphorosis Magazine
Plant Based Press
Verdage
Vestige

You can also find us:
Metaphorosis@writing.exchange
@Metaphorosis
www.facebook.com/metaphorosis

Help keep Metaphorosis running by supporting us at
Patreon.com/metaphorosis

See more about some of our books on the following pages.

Metaphorosis Magazine

Metaphorosis

a magazine of speculative fiction

Metaphorosis is an online speculative fiction magazine dedicated to quality writing. We publish an original story every week, along with author bios, interviews, and notes on story origins.

We also publish monthly print and e-book issues, as well as yearly Best of and Complete anthologies.

Come and see us online at magazine.Metaphorosis.com.

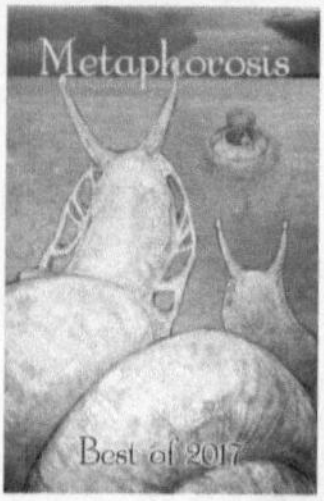

Plant Based Press

plant
based
press

Vegan-friendly science fiction and fantasy, including anthologies of the year's best SFF stories, from 2016-2020.

Chambers of the Heart

speculative stories
by
B. Morris Allen

A heart that's a building, a dog that's a program, a woman sinking irretrievably — stories about love, loss, and motion.

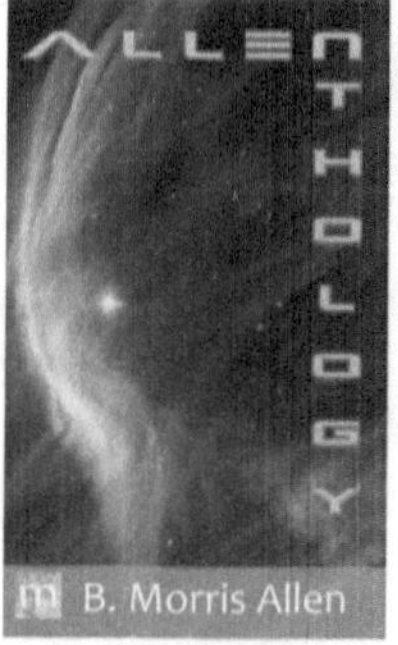

Susurrus

A darkly romantic story of magic, love, and suffering.

Allenthology: Volume I

Including three full collections of SFF stories.

Verdage

Science fiction and fantasy books for writers — full of great stories, often with an additional focus on the craft of speculative fiction writing.

Reading 5X5 x3

Changes

How do stories move from 'maybe' to published?

Here are 15 case studies of stories published in *Metaphorosis* magazine.

Reading 5X5 x2

Duets

How do authors' voices change when they collaborate?

A round-robin of five talented science fiction and fantasy authors collaborating with each other and writing solo.

Including stories by Evan Marcroft, David Gallay, J. Tynan Burke, L'Erin Ogle, and Douglas Anstruther.

Score

an SFF symphony

An anthology with an emotional score from the heights of joy to the depths of despair – but always with a little hope shining through.

Reading 5X5

Five stories, five times

See how different writers take on the same material.

Reading 5X5

Writers' Edition

Two extra stories, the story seed, and authors' notes on writing.

Vestige

Novelettes, novellas, and novels by Metaphorosis authors.

The Nocturnals
Mariah Montoya

Night is Dangerous. Day is deadly.

Where day and night last thirty years, humans move constantly stay ahead of the night and cruel Nocturnals that call it home. But a boy is lost out there.

www.ingramcontent.com/pod-product-compliance
Lightning Source LLC
Chambersburg PA
CBHW032307070726

47590CB00015B/869